BAD HOUSES

BAD HOUSES

Stories
John Elizabeth Stintzi

ARSENAL PULP PRESS
VANCOUVER

ARSENAL PULP PRESS
Suite 202 – 211 East Georgia St.
Vancouver, BC V6A 1Z6
Canada
arsenalpulp.com

The publisher gratefully acknowledges the support of the Canada Council for the Arts and the
British Columbia Arts Council for its publishing program and the Government of Canada and
the Government of British Columbia (through the Book Publishing Tax Credit Program) for its
publishing activities.

Arsenal Pulp Press acknowledges the xʷməθkʷəy̓əm (Musqueam), Sḵwx̱wú7mesh (Squamish),
and səlilwətaɬ (Tsleil-Waututh) Nations, custodians of the traditional, ancestral, and unceded
territories where our office is located. We pay respect to their histories, traditions, and continuous
living cultures and commit to accountability, respectful relations, and friendship.

This is a work of fiction. Any resemblance of characters to persons either living or deceased is
purely coincidental.

The following stories were previously published in different form: "Dumb House" in *The Humber
Literary Review*, volume 2, issue 3 (fall + winter 2016/17); "Elephant" in *Minola Review*, issue 31
(September 2021); "Pathetic Fallacy" in *Hobart* (May 3, 2019); "Moving Parts" in *Plenitude*
(May 8, 2021).

Cover design by John Elizabeth Stintzi
Text design by Jazmin Welch
Edited by Catharine Chen
Proofread by Alison Strobel

Printed and bound in Canada

Library and Archives Canada Cataloguing in Publication:
Title: Bad houses : stories / John Elizabeth Stintzi.
Names: Stintzi, John Elizabeth, author.
Identifiers: Canadiana (print) 20240317270 | Canadiana (ebook) 20240317289 |
    ISBN 9781551529615 (softcover) | ISBN 9781551529622 (EPUB)
Subjects: LCGFT: Short stories.
Classification: LCC PS8637.T55 B33 2024 | DDC C813/.6—dc23

To Axel B. Kolcow, the eternal champion of my tales

So maybe there's this moment. It's different for everyone, but it's pivotal. It's the moment your head gets screwed off and screwed on again, and everything is changed forever. You can never see life the same way again. You can never go back.

—KAREN TEI YAMASHITA, *I Hotel*

In short, hell.

—MIKHAIL BULGAKOV, *The Master and Margarita*

CONTENTS

DUMB HOUSE

ONE DAY OUR ROOMMATE CAME HOME, painted her face white, and stopped speaking. She piled all her chromatic clothes in a hamper outside her door, and the next day, after dragging them three blocks to a thrift shop, came back to the house with bags of new clothes. Everything was white and black. Every shirt was striped. Our other roommate and I confronted her as she was carrying those bags into the house. We asked her what she was doing. She didn't respond; she just stared at us, a perfectly shaped, big black-painted tear ever dripping from the far corner of her left eye. Her hair, newly dyed jet black, was stuffed up into a small beret.

She put down her bags and lifted her hands out to the space between herself and us and began patting at the gap. It was solid. There was an invisible barrier. We watched as she inspected the entirety of the hall, running her hands from edge to edge, floor to ceiling. Finding no gaps, her face went somehow more blank as she began to beat her fists on the thick space. Her hands bruised, but she couldn't break through. She started trying to push the wall. Her feet slipped on the floor behind her. We took a few steps back and the invisible wall followed us, with her still pushing at it. We didn't reach out to touch the wall. Not then, and not for a while. We preferred to think about the wall as performance rather than reality. So we stepped back until she'd pushed it far enough that she could get into her room. At that point, she stopped pushing, caught her breath, picked up the bags of clothes, and carried them inside.

She was still paying rent, at first, but she'd stopped going to work. She'd been interning for a literary agency for a few months, since Christmas. She would read what the agents had agreed to look at personally; she knew what they would feel was worthy. She grabbed coffee, schmoozed authors who were writing real books that real people might eventually read and and whose manuscripts circumvented her. She ordered new business cards for everyone in the agency. She ordered business cards for herself that had no position title except "Writer." She wasn't even writing anymore.

We scoured her social media. We were trying to figure it all out. She hadn't tweeted, her LinkedIn account was deactivated, and we couldn't find her OkCupid, where we would occasionally sign on to tease one another, to fake-flirt as characters who were clearly serial killers trying to lure their next kills. We could no longer tell her that she'd love our basement because it was so erotically dark. The profile pic on all her remaining social media accounts changed. In this new monochromatic photo, she stared deep into the camera. The camera stared back into her. But even in that photo, the thick invisible wall was deepening the picture's flatness.

She stopped leaving poems on the fridge for us, poems that admitted her guilt at finishing the last of my milk or pillaging two of our roommate's oranges. No more poems that began, "This Is Just to Say." She stopped retaliating our playfully aggressive good night wishes, never again kicked in the bathroom door when I was brushing my teeth at night to grab me by the shoulders and tell me to go clam-shut my lids and *fucking dream*. She stopped inviting people over or really ever leaving her room much at all. Sometimes we'd come back from work, from our own internships at publishing houses that kept us from doing our own writing, and she'd be sitting in the middle of the living room, panicking as the invisible boundaries of a box began closing in on her. We would watch the invisible flatness compress her skin. Eventually, the box would ease, let her free, and she would go back into her bedroom, shaking. When she cried, she cried silently. Her breaths were light and liquid.

She passed along the edges of our lives like a ghost. Her wake smelled of paint and baby powder. She never again sneezed or coughed or sang.

A few weeks in, she got some new business cards made. They arrived at our house, and she was silent but excited. All of her expressions had become visibly—almost comically—exaggerated. We watched her open the package from the other side of the living room, so as not to closet her in. She unpacked the box of cards and pulled a few out and smiled. She'd painted a black smile on her face that morning and had made the black tear somewhat smaller than usual, down from nickel-diameter to dime. She began to cry, exaggeratedly and with dry eyes, while her painted face kept smiling. Then she came toward us, one white-gloved hand in front of her as if she were navigating a half-familiar dark, reaching for the invisible wall so she wouldn't crash into it. After she found it, she knelt and placed two of her business cards face down on the floor, then slunk back to her bedroom, stepping over invisible obstacles, with the box of cards stuffed under her arm. She closed her door. We went up to the cards and picked them up. We flipped them over. They were completely blank.

Soon after that, her rent stopped coming. We saw her even less. On his days off, my other roommate would sit at the top of the stairs that led up to his bedroom to see if she ever came out to eat. She didn't. Once when I was walking home, I spotted her sitting at her window, staring out into the clouds, lowering her hand into a bowl and lifting to her painted mouth nothing. She chewed the nothing thoroughly and swallowed. A few days later, I caught her in the kitchen trying to gouge new holes into her black-leather belt with a corkscrew.

One morning not long after that, I had to go to work without showering because there was an invisible wall in front of the shower. I'd hit my nose on it and bled. Later that day, my other roommate needed help carrying a bookcase he'd bought at a yard sale up the stairway to his room, but as soon as I grabbed my end and he his, the bookcase wouldn't move at all. It was stuck, still in the air. We traced our hands along the wood until we found the invisible wall that was bisecting the bookcase. It was six inches deep. I took a few steps back and watched him drag the bookcase up the stairs himself, banging and gouging the wood as it went.

A few months in, the landlord knocked on our door. When I opened it, I discovered that he was not knocking on the door, but instead on an invisible barrier three feet in front of it. He tried to talk to me, but the wall was so thick that all his yelling was muffled. I made a gesture with open palms and my shoulders as if to say, "I can't understand you." He pulled a small notebook from his pocket, wrote YOU GUYS OWE in large letters across a two-page spread, and stuck it up against the wall. Slowly, the wall started pushing him back. Which only made him more furious. Which only made it push him faster, all the way back into the street, where he would've been hit by a speeding car, had it not crashed into another immovable wall to the landlord's right. The landlord was safe in a tightening box, reddening with rage. I left him to it and went back inside, to my room. I wanted to write for the first time in a very long time, but I couldn't get to my computer. I turned my back to the barrier and looked out the window, noticing that the landlord had escaped and was kicking his way down the street. But the man whose car had hit the wall was standing on the sidewalk now. His car was in the middle of the street, crushed into a perfect cube of wreck, shrinking. The man looked like he was screaming, but I couldn't hear him. He was reddening too.

Our roommate painted more tears under her eyes, while we went out and got extra jobs to supplement the minimum wage of our internships in an attempt to cover her rent. I started installing drywall on weekends. My other roommate started selling high-end baby carriages door to door. When I came home I was coated in white dust from the gypsum. When he came home he was sunburnt with a crick in his back. Our roommate never left the house anymore. At some point her bedroom door had busted off its hinges, so he or I would sometimes stand on the other side of the living room and watch her with his binoculars—one at a time, so as not to box each other in. We were afraid of getting close, to her and to each other. We moved around the house as three opposing poles.

We began to resent her. We both worked more and more while she sat in her room with her doorway wide open, silently braiding invisible ropes while calculating with a notepad the cubic feet of the box around her. I tried, with the binoculars, to read the solutions to her equations, but I couldn't. The angle wasn't quite right.

Once, with the binoculars, I watched her using some of her rope to make a pair of invisible suspenders. Her belt had gotten too loose again, and the corkscrew was too far away and surrounded by too many walls. I didn't tell our other roommate about that. He never told me how he watched her paint her face—not until after, years after, when we met over coffee and talked it all out. He said that she'd painted her face completely black first, then gone over it again and again with white, leaving only the left-eye tear and sometimes—though more and more rarely—the smile. But even then, I didn't tell him about the belt. When we were finished I tried to reach for the bill, but it was on his side of a very thin wall.

The landlord called us. The landlord emailed us. We sent him cheques but he never cashed them. On the phone, when he got through, he said he couldn't get to his goddamned mailbox at all, for the immense nothing surrounding it. We tried wiring him the money. It took six tries and eventually it worked, but by then it was too late. We were too poor and too far behind, and he wanted us out. I texted both of my roommates—one had not texted me in six days, the other hadn't texted me in over three months. Neither responded, though my other roommate's things began to disappear from the house that day. By that night he was completely gone. After he left, I stood in our old corner, watching my roommate in her room with his binoculars, which he'd forgotten to take. She was sitting in her invisible box. It was getting smaller. She had given up scribbling figures and could hardly move around for the spools of invisible rope she'd made. But she'd propped the notebook against the far wall of the box, and finally I could see the equations. The solutions for volume, for the rate of its shrinking.

In the margins were formulas for force.

That night, while I was packing up my things in my room, I heard a muted sound of metal being ground. I went to the kitchen corner and saw her sitting in a sea of sparks, sharpening some invisible tool with an invisible spinning grindstone. I watched for a while as the sparks burned, embedding themselves in the walls of the box. They hung there, glinting for a moment until burning out. Eventually, I went to bed and had nightmares about drywall. I had nightmares about being an intern forever. About never writing another word. My nightmares were punctuated by the sound of shattering glass.

I woke up very early the following morning. It was too quiet. I went to the kitchen and picked up the binoculars, but I didn't see my roommate in her room. She was no longer in the box. I went into her room, crawling, feeling for the invisible box, and cut my hand open on a broken shard of it. My blood dripped down and the pieces took shape, scattered along the floor where she'd busted through. But the tail end of her thick rope also took shape, and I followed it out of the room. With my sliced hand I smeared a crimson line, mapping out its concrete absence. It led me outside and down the street in the cool early morning. I was light-headed by the time I got to the end of it, almost a quarter mile away, in the middle of a park whose trees cushioned the sounds of the loudest part of the city. It was quiet there but for birds screeching in the trees and garbage trucks crushing trash as they trundled down the nearby avenues, leaving plastic bins tipped over in their wake. There, in that park, hanging from a low, bent bough of a brittle-boned tree, our roommate spun, suspended by nothing, imprisoned by the black and white bars of her shirt.

There were no more tears painted on her face. Or, as I would learn years later, there was no more face painted around her tears. Her face was a simple slate of black. It twisted in the wind. The wind was quiet. The wind was cool.

GRAMPA'S BAG OF
BUBONIC'S BROOD

WHEN I FEEL BAD, I play with my Jesus action figure. Then I feel less bad, and I start to feel sorry. Sorry for yelling at my gramma and calling her names under my breath after being talked to for letting another dish rot in my bedroom. Sorry for laughing at a neighbour kid falling in the street. Sorry for lying. When I play with my Jesus action figure, I feel goodness coming into my body from him, because my Jesus action figure has real sin-cleansing action. Which means that whenever I touch him against people, they start to shine. They turn good.

But he hasn't always had that power. He didn't have that power when my grampa gave him to me last Easter, after the bunny forgot to come barf his eggs up on our lawn. The day before Mom left. My Jesus got the power when I took him to church a week later and tried to drown him in a bowl of holy water after the service was done and everyone was in the basement eating slices of lemon bread and drinking cups of His blood. I was angry at Jesus for reasons I don't need to get into, them being in the past, and I decided Jesus was going to get drowned for them. I was a different kid back then.

Of course Jesus can't drown, even in action figure form. He is not a bag of kittens, like the one my grampa drowned down in the river where I saw a cottonmouth swim around once. He drowned those kittens the day before I tried to drown Jesus. I was with my grampa when he did it. I am not saying that one of the reasons that convinced me Jesus was a bad guy who deserved drowning was making kittens too expensive to keep alive, but the fact is they are. That's just the fact.

I learned even more especially that Jesus definitely can't be drowned in holy water. When I tried, it only made him stronger, so that now he cleanses sins. After a bit of being submersed in the holy water, he got his sin-cleansing powers and made me good, and since good kids don't drown Jesus, I stopped drowning him. Now I'm good. But the goodness does tend to wear off, and I've got to re-cleanse now and again, badness being a hard thing to permanently lose.

I took my sin-cleansing Jesus home with me that day after church. My gramparents were next door for after-church tea with the neighbours, so my sister was the only one home when I got back, herself having slipped out of church early to watch daytime TV with people screaming at each other and calling each other bad, as she usually did. Those kinds of shows relaxed her. Made her feel more okay. My sister was just sitting on the couch, popping bubble gum she'd stolen a few days before. I walked over to her and placed the head of Jesus on her forehead.

We shared a bedroom then, and we share a new bedroom now, but back then, when pissed at me, which was fairly often, she liked to pick her boogers and put them on my headboard because it grossed me out so bad. But at Jesus's action touch, all of a sudden her green eyes blew wide, and she glowed, and she said: "I'm sorry, Michael, and Jesus, for all the boogers!" Then she took the gum out of her mouth, moulded it into a cube, wrapped it back up in its crumply paper, and put it back in the package. She got up from the permanent depression of the couch. She was going to take it all the way back to the store. Not that it was far.

So she went, and when she got back, our gramparents still weren't back. She went to our bedroom and pried all her boogers off of my headboard with a butter knife and then came and started begging at my feet for forgiveness. She became like a different person. I told her it was okay, Jesus in hand. I was a bad brother to her before too, though I was ten (not eleven, like now) and she seven, and nobody could have expected me or her to be very saintly at such innocent, unwise ages.

I told her I was sorry too, because I was. I told her I was sorry for telling Gramma that she was hiding under the porch after Mom left and for that one time I climbed into her bed, months before, and told her about my body and what I'd just learned to do with it. It was like magic, and she was fascinated too, and wasn't making like it was a sin. It didn't feel like one until my Jesus action figure cleansed me. Then I knew that what I had been doing was really, really bad. But being good is just knowing what you've done is bad and feeling bad about it. And now when I get those weird lonely feelings, or feelings like I should go and share some of the mysteries of my body with my sister, because I want someone to know with me, I go and grab my Jesus action figure, and he re-cleanses me and makes me feel bad about feeling that way. And now, thanks to the occasional re-cleansing of Jesus, my sister doesn't have any more boogers, boogers being a side effect of being a sinful person.

Mom left before I could bring Jesus to her. She needed him, and she called out to him a lot in anger. Jesus Christ this, Jesus Christ that! Perhaps that was why Grampa had got me the action figure, thinking I could help Mom. Well, I could've helped Mom, but she wasn't around to be helped anymore. She left Easter Sunday after the bunny skipped us, and Grampa gave me this soon-to-be sin-cleansing Jesus and gave my sister an ordinary ostrich doll.

Mom left a day before Jesus was supposed to have risen out of the dirt or knocked on the door of the casket or whatever it is he did. I think the Bible says differently than our church, which every year has a silent play during a long prayer involving a guy with a beard being nailed into a casket and Mary and some disciples sitting around pretending to be very sad. Then, at the end of the praying, at "Amen," the guy in the casket knocks on it, and all the players realize that Jesus is actually inside the box that they had before believed empty, that being how religion works. After a few fetch their crowbars, they break him out, and Jesus puts a halo hat on his head that he was keeping in his white robe, puts his hands together, and starts leading another prayer. Every year I'm surprised.

Gramma and Grampa were around visiting us when Mom left, so they stayed on, trying to figure out what to do. We didn't know what we were supposed to do about Mom, and even now we don't, because she still hasn't come back. But now we are living at Gramma and Grampa's, which is two-and-a-half miles away from our old house and smaller. My sister is still waiting, but I am too stuck in my holy work to try and get into the waiting business. I sometimes disappear for a whole day, trying to get people to become good, cleansing and re-cleansing. Knocking on doors. I tell my sister I will start to wait for Mom only when I hear her knocking on the door. I will start to wait when I can see her walking up to me, and I'll wait while she say things. But until then, I don't have the ability to just wait for something that I can't see coming. Even if I believe that it is.

Mom's leaving was always an occasional thing that I was used to anyway, though this last time was the first our gramparents ever heard of it. But me and my sister were distracted from this leaving at first because Bubonic, the local she-cat, had birthed a litter of five kittens in our house. Bubonic was a cat we'd never owned but let inside on most days, especially in the summer when we were around all the time to watch her. Me and my sister always loved her. She had a fun way of biting when she was sick of belly rubs that didn't hurt too much, and she had extra toes that meant she was probably lucky. She could be seen most nights scrounging in the dump or in the open bins of trash outside peoples' houses for scraps of food and leftovers unspooned from tin cans.

The first time I saw her, I was six, and she was pretty little and had a tomato sauce can stuck on her head. She was walking down along the street, swinging her head back and forth. I got it off of her and she seemed happy about that. She stank of tomatoes and trash. She was really thankful and friendly.

Most days she'd come into our house to sleep in safety from Ruffo. Ruffo was a local dog that showed up some time after Bubonic, and he swung his head down the street, slobbering, without the help of any cans. He too was mostly wild but a tad tame, and unlike Bubonic he had nowhere to be during the day but was gone in the night. Ruffo wasn't a fan of cats, and he didn't bite fun. Once he chased me because he thought I had a sandwich and nearly nipped my bare leg. No matter how many times I touch Ruffo with Jesus, smacking him across the face with him as he salivates along after me, he has never got good.

Bubonic had her kittens in me and my sisters' room, under my sister's bed, because my sister had a tendency of kicking her dirty clothes there. It became a nice nest for Bubonic, and when my sister was upset, it was one of her own favourite spots to hide. She, like Mom, also has a tendency of disappearing, but hers happen only when she is sad or angry, or scared, which is kind of both. The difference with my sister is I can always find her. Once she even hid in the refrigerator, which I discovered because she had taken out the shelves and put them on the counter, stacked next to some really gross-smelling mouldy things Mom had left. I opened the door and she almost fell out, for all the shivering, and I told her she was dumb and carried her, her teeth chattering, to bed and lay next to her for a few hours to help warm her up.

That was the longest time Mom had gone before now, about five full days. When she came back we always pretended like nothing happened. We'd say things like "Good morning, Mommy," and try our best not to run at her right off and hug her and love her and spook her away again. She would always kiss us on the head and only ever did that when she'd come back. While she was gone, we kept Bubonic in the house all night long, and we slept together in the same bed.

On the third day of that five-day period, I went to a friend's house to play with him, and when we played hide-and-seek, he hid, and before I seeked, I stole food from his kitchen. Half a loaf of bread and two cans of beans and a few apples, which would turn out not to be enough. I feel pretty bad about stealing that food now that I have Jesus, and I did go apologize a few days after Jesus got his powers. But back then, before, I didn't feel bad, I just put the food in my burlap knapsack, which my gramma sewed together for me from a burlap sack and ropes. She said it would last me years and that she herself had that sort of thing when she was my age. Did they even have burlap back then? But it did last me a while, at least until my grampa mistakened it for just any old burlap sack.

My sister found Bubonic's kittens because she was pulling out her dirty clothes for Gramma to wash. We hadn't yet realized that Mom had run off again, but our gramparents had caught wind of it, I think, between Gramma's sneezes from her being allergic to cats. I figure they were trying to busy us so we'd keep not noticing, thinking it was unusual for her to go. Grampa told me to mow the front lawn, so at the time I was mowing, with my powerless Jesus action figure peeking out of my pocket, and I was thinking about Jesus himself knocking on his coffin, letting people know that he's exactly where they don't expect him to be. But then my sister ran out and grabbed me by the arm and said, "There are cat babies under my bed!"

There were five of them. Like Bubonic, three of them were black tabby, and two were fully stone grey. They had little blue eyes that were, at that point, barely squints. Bubonic wasn't too happy we found her, but seemed to be understanding and proud of her little brood of kittens. They were suckling on her hard, and for most of the time they didn't really do much else besides sleep. Me and my sister, with the lawn half-cut and her clothes half-pulled from under the bed and our mom gone, had stiff necks the next morning because we spent so long on our bellies, necks bent up, watching the kittens and Bubonic.

At breakfast the next day, while Gramma was blowing her nose and rubbing her red eyes, we realized Mom was gone again because it was Easter Monday, and that seemed like an important time to be together. Me and my sister weren't sure how to take it. I'd never been to the service and seen Jesus knock on the coffin without her, so I expected her to show back up.

Me and my sister dressed up for church and every now and again looked under the bed at Bubonic and the kittens. Bubonic was pretty squinty too, tired out but happy. I left her some leftover sloppy meat to eat on the floor by the bed, along with a little bowl of water. Me and my sister were happy about the kittens, but were a bit at throats over them because we both had different ideas of who should get which. There were too many, or too few, to split down the middle, and the only way that made sense was to have one of us get the black tabbies and one of us get the greys. One of us could have gotten Bubonic, but we decided that she didn't count. She was the world's. Neither of us wanted to get fewer kittens, but my sister was so insistent about it, and so I got the greys. But I wasn't happy about it. I wanted to get three things to name.

During the service at the church, me and my sister sat between our gramparents, and I thought of names for the grey kittens. We'd named Bubonic that because Mom at the beginning was warning us that she would give us bubonic flu if we played with her, so when we played with her and started to love her, we took bubonic flu to be that and named her after it. But this time I got to name the kittens without Mom's influence. While the praying was happening and the silent play was going on, I thought Coffin would be a good name for one of them, as one of my grey cats, the runt, liked to just lie there and sleep a lot and then suddenly wake up and thrash around, mewing for Bubonic, while the other liked to wander around, eyes closed. That one I decided to call Explorer. Then Gramma sneezed through the quiet just as Jesus knocked on the lid of his coffin. "Hey, let me out." I was surprised again, as ever, at the good-as-gone coming back. Even when I knew it was coming. My Jesus action figure, powerless, sat in my shirt pocket. Mom wasn't there. The crowbars came out. A halo hat got pulled from a robe.

My sister was slow about coming up with her names. She said she wanted to be sure about them, that she wanted them to be based on personality, like Coffin's and Explorer's. She was slow because I could tell she was starting to get a bit distracted by Mom being gone. I saw her start to sort of look about for places to stash herself, as I'd seen her do a lot in the past. I didn't think much about Mom being gone, as I'm older and more mature. More used to it, I guess. But I've also always believed she was coming back, and my sister never had that sort of belief. When I was seven once I went to a week-long summer camp and had to be brought home after three days because my sister freaked out so much about having lost her brother forever, and hid herself underneath the neighbour's car and almost got run over when they pulled out to drive to the store. Of course I'd missed her too.

By the end of the second week, when Mom still wasn't back, my sister still hadn't named her kittens, and my grampa had me put them all in my burlap knapsack. On the way to the river my grampa had me carry a big rock from the backyard as an anchor, which was a rock I had actually hand-picked for Mom from a gravel pit near the dump. It had crystals on its surface, and some-day I wanted to buy a big hammer and break into it to see if it had diamonds inside. At the edge of the river I put the rock in the bag, and he threw it into the water. We weren't there for longer than a few minutes. He brought me with him when he did it. My sister had hidden herself during the night and didn't know what was going on. She had been hiding in different places for the last week, and I knew where she was hiding that time. I saw her toes poking out from a pile of towels in the bathroom closet when I went in to pee just after I'd bagged up the kittens and before I'd gotten the rock. I didn't give away her position because I knew she was running out of places that our gramparents didn't know to check. They've never understood my sister.

Me and grampa walked to the river, which wasn't too far, with the knapsack full of the kittens. Of course Bubonic wasn't in the bag, but she was following us, mewing loud and wanting the kit-tens back. I didn't tell grampa that the sack we were using was the burlap knapsack that gramma made me for school, because he had a tendency to get angry at people when he thought they were trying to stop him from doing something he'd been considering doing for a long time. He is a nice man, but he's hard. He came into me and my sister's bedroom that morning and walked over to me and simply said, "We are taking the kittens to the river." He held out my bag to me. "Put them in here."

On the way to the river my grampa told me about money. He said some people got it, some people don't, and some people have so little that they don't even have the luxury of having no money, but instead they owe it to people. He said, "Michael, your mom is one of these people, and I guess we have to deal with that now that she's left. We're going to sell the house and take you kids to our place. We can barely afford to keep you two fed, let alone kittens. And anyway, your gramma is allergic, and though she can't help that, we can. Not in an easy way." He paused as we reached the river and looked over to me. "And it's not fair to any of them to be left to the elements. They'll just die slower and more painfully. They just won't last, they're not built for that kind of life."

I didn't look at him while he was talking, I was looking in the river, where I'd seen that cottonmouth swimming around after a small school of minnow fish a year or so before, thinking about it coming around again to try and go after the cats in my knapsack. I can still remember the way it was swimming, a squiggle dark as sin.

The river was flowing a bit and the rock was heavy in my hands. Grampa held the bag and the kittens were loud and Bubonic was mewing and climbing up grampa's leg, claws latching to his trousers, long nipples rubbing milk stains into the fabric. She just wanted them back, no matter what, knowing that they needed her. I still remember how their fur felt against the backs of my hands when I had to lower that big rock into the bag, moving the kittens to either side so as not to crush them with it. Coffin, Explorer, and the three unnamed. I didn't watch when grampa threw them in the water, but I did hear the splash, and saw the ripples hit our bank, where my feet were sunk in mud. I wouldn't have been surprised had the ripples kept going, from the water over me and all along the land, small ridged waves knocking over potted plants and empty cups. I was crouching with Bubonic, watching her eyes follow the bag in. I'd forgotten Jesus on my bed.

So when I got back, I was pretty upset. Bubonic didn't follow us, she sat beside the river, mewing, waiting for the kittens to come back. On the walk I just thought, why is it that good kittens, coming from a good cat, couldn't make it just because of money and allergies? Why is here so bad for them to be able to grow up right? I got angry about that, being at the cusp of my wisdom. I felt that was unfair. I was angry, but I wasn't angry at Grampa, because he knew what he was doing and had considered it from all the angles, like he always did. And because I knew that he wasn't happy about it either. He was walking home quicker and stiffer than me.

When I went into my bedroom I saw my sister's bare feet sticking out from under my bed and found Jesus by my pillow. I had been sleeping with him by my side. I took him and I knocked him off the bed and sat on it, slowly, so as not to scare my sister. I looked down and she was wiggling her toes. I remember thinking then that maybe my sister hides so that I can always find her.

"Where'd the babies go?" she asked. I stared down at the toes and caught a tear in my fist before it could hit them. I took a breath.

"We took them to live at the dump," I said, lying down. "We're going to live at Gramma and Grampa's place, Grampa says. There's no way we can keep the kittens there, since Gramma is so allergic. Besides, they're a litter. They're supposed to be at the dump." My face was wet and my sister stayed under the bed. "But I can take you to go visit them, if you want."

That afternoon me and my sister went to the dump to try and find the kittens, but we couldn't. We looked in the tub of an old washing machine and in the wheel well of an abandoned rusty car. I told her that Grampa told me cats will sometimes hide their kittens when they know people have figured out where they are, so that's probably what Bubonic did. We walked back, and my sister was still trying to come up with names for her cats. Spunky. Sport. Tiffany. Sneezles. They were many and all wrong.

When we got back to the house, Gramma and Grampa had started packing up our stuff. We were going to leave in the next few days. On that Sunday morning Bubonic showed up at our door, breasts plump and wailing. I scared her off with a broom, and then Ruffo came scampering out of a yard and took after her, his drool mouth convincing her to leave. Grampa was up and drinking coffee when I got back with the broom. Then we woke up my sister again and went to church, and I tried to drown Jesus, and I became a new, good kid. Then I fixed my sister with him, and when my gramparents came back I touched them with Jesus too, and they too became good, little beams of light dancing around them both. Between Gramma's sneezes, they started to apologize to each other for all sorts of bad things they'd done, and to us for the things they'd done toward us that were less than good, like when Gramma hit me in the head with a stick when I was being silly.

That evening we started driving our stuff to their house. Grampa never said sorry for the kittens, not even after I re-cleansed him weeks later, when I sat beside him on the couch while he was watching a plane-fighting show on the History channel. I sat beside him and stared at the TV for a few moments and then gently tapped him on the arm with Jesus, watching the sparks of his power jump onto Grampa's skin. He looked over and took Jesus from me, looking down at him as a Spitfire was spit out of the air on the TV. He stared Jesus in the eyes, and I was hoping he was going to ask for forgiveness then. Even though it wasn't his fault, I wanted him to feel bad about the kittens. But instead he asked me where I got the toy, as he'd forgotten that he gave it to me around Easter. I told him that I found it by the road, and as soon as he handed the toy back to me, I got bathed in the sin-cleansing action and apologized for lying, and told him the truth.

My sister seems different now that I've been fixing her of her sins. She seems happy. But I'm not happy. I've been holding back the one thing that is keeping me from being perfectly good from the start: that I lied to my sister about the kittens.

But I've kept that to myself because I think it's better this way. I'll always be a small sinner, and not even my Jesus's real sin-cleansing action is strong enough to make me change that decision and hurt her. But I still feel bad about it, like Jesus makes me feel about my other sins, which I make amends for. But I don't regret it. Nowadays I go around on my own time and ask people if they want to be good, and some of them say sure and so I give them a treatment of Jesus's sin-cleansing touch and make them good, and some say no, and I don't touch them with him. I figured I can't impress Jesus's sin-cleansing action without someone letting me. I don't charge for the service, but still most people say no when I ask them. Not many people around here want to be good. One man said to me, "If I were good I'd probably end up broke or dead—can't afford it, kid." One person who chose to be good I heard tried to break up a bar fight in the city and got stitches. My teacher told me to stop bringing Jesus to school.

Since we moved to our gramparents' place, I have come back to our old house and waited nearby for Bubonic. I carry Jesus in my pocket like a gun in a Western and wear a wooden cross under my shirt. I go back to the house because I want to apologize to Bubonic and also because I want to make my mom good if she just happens to come back when I'm there. But I'm only waiting for Bubonic. I only saw Bubonic once, far down the street. I ran at her but she disappeared into some brush by the time I got close. Mom hasn't come back yet.

I'm waiting at the house right now. I just turned eleven years old and am getting sick of the guilt that Jesus has given me due to his closeness and my not wanting to tell my sister the truth about the kittens. I haven't seen Bubonic yet today, and the sun is getting ready to go down. I am tired of waiting, and I decide to go down to the river before I walk back, so I go. I haven't been there since I went down with Grampa. On the way there I whistle and keep on the lookout. For cats or snakes.

When I get to the river I find that it's shallower than it was the last time I came. It has been a dry year. I take Jesus, with his sin-cleansing action, out of my pocket and look at his little plastic face with his little plastic beard, and how the paint of his robes has started to scratch off. His left arm is loose in its socket, probably from all the good he's done. Holy light squiggles up my arm from his plastic fingertips like cartoon electrics, and I feel bad still, again, if not worse. It's funny how ashamed he makes me feel, sort of like the same amount of feeling I had when I decided to drown him in the holy water.

In the river I see some more ripples, and looking, I see that it's there, swimming around again near the surface: the cottonmouth, wriggling through the water's midsummer dark. Maybe it's not the same one, but he's swimming through the muddy river the same.

His movement is so easy, and I hate him, and I decide I also hate my Jesus action figure, and that hate feels bad because holding on to him forces me to be good. So I wind up my arm and pitch Jesus into the water. The cottonmouth swims away, afraid, up the other bank and into the underbrush. The muddy water clears a bit around the sinking Jesus. It brightens. For a moment it's like there's a sun diving into the water. But then it darkens, and the water gets muddy again.

From my bank, more ripples come. I take a step back, then turn and run from the five skeletal kittens who are rising proudly from the swill. Jesus is riding the second one, the runt Coffin, and he's kicking its sides with his feet and raising his right hand to me, shooting out light like laser beams. His left arm hangs limply as he rides.

As I run I can feel their dead bones mewing, calling, following me. I can feel the wooden cross knock against my chest at every bound. Beams of spreading goodness whiz past me and pop in the air and on the gravel path, blasting little holes in front of my feet. My lungs burn as I pull out onto the road and keep running, not looking back, believing that he must have given up chase by now. Houses go past me, the church does, the store. I tell myself I don't see the light anymore and think how even when Jesus isn't in my hand, or in my pocket holster, that even when he's galloping along far behind me and shooting his light at me, I'm still somehow ashamed. Especially as his beams begin to land in my back.

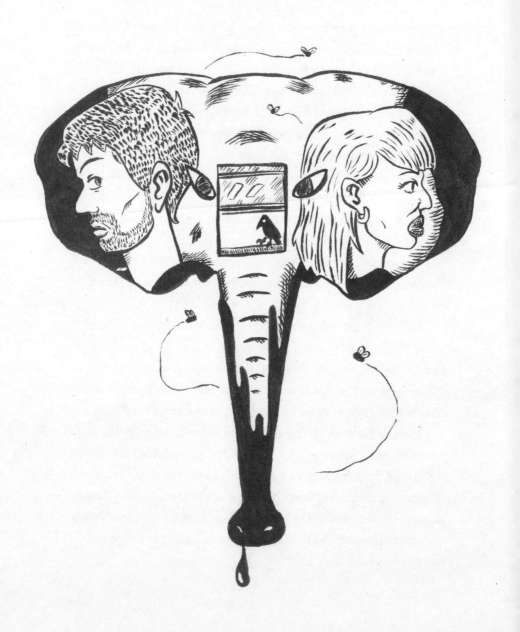

ELEPHANT

one

The morning after, there was an elephant in the tiny studio apartment, lying across the queen-size bed. The young man was sleeping on the floor beside the door, and the young woman was sprawled out, snoring, by the stove. The young man woke up first, as he always did, only this time he had to pull one of her brown leather boots from his cheek. He was naked. He always slept naked. He stood up and turned around in the tiny apartment as the elephant let out a final breath and then defecated all over the bed and along the floor—nearly splashing him. He could barely manoeuvre himself around the elephant and its mess in the tiny apartment to get to where she was, near the stove and also the window, which he crammed himself toward, between the elephant and the wall, then opened full-wide to let all the stale air out. Then he put the coffee on, and the zoo smell of elephant shit mingled with the smell of fresh cheap brew. He stood by the stove looking at her sleep, watching the elephant, waiting for it to breathe. He looked at her only long enough to see if she was still there, still wearing her underwear, still asleep. When the coffee maker beeped, she woke up and he stopped looking at her, and he drank the coffee black because he didn't want to try to get to the fridge, because all the fresh air was where he was, by the coffee maker. She sat up with her back to the stove and asked him if the elephant was dead, and he said it wasn't, not at first—at first it was alive, then it died and shit all over the room. She began to run her hands through her hair, wondering if she could get away with not showering before work, and deciding that she could. He was still naked. He couldn't get away with that, though he also didn't work. She got up, went to the closet, got dressed, spun around in the one or two square feet of clear floor, and left. When she was gone, he put down his coffee and crawled onto the elephant, opened its huge eyelid, put his head against its huge chest, and listened for its huge heart, which didn't beat, then slithered down the huge belly, landing and slipping on some shit, busting his bare ass, stinking. But he made his way to his chest of drawers, though due to the splay of the elephant's foot far beyond the reaches of the bed, he couldn't open the drawer that held his socks and underwear. So he put on pants and a T-shirt and shoes, grabbed his laptop, and went down to the café at the corner to write.

two

They lived like that, with the dead elephant dominating the apartment, blocking her cellphone charger, blocking his sock drawer, for weeks. He got blisters, she missed calls. With the window of the apartment still open, the cool air kept the elephant from rotting too fast, though of course it still did. The grey skin whitened and tightened with stiffening bloat, and carrion birds perched outside the window screen. She named the quiet buzzards and hated the magpies. He loved the crows, but he also cursed them, how their presence alongside the ravens blurred his perceptions, in the same way that he cursed his friend who, over the phone, tried to sympathize with him by telling him the story about the bull that he and his girlfriend had caught stomping china plates in their kitchen one day, how they had to herd it down five flights of stairs, he baiting it with a red tablecloth, she prodding it with a barbecue spatula, until it was finally out in the streets and free of them. "We can't herd the dead elephant out of the apartment, the door's too small," the young man told his friend, the clothespin on his nose permanently changing the shape of both his nostrils and his voice. That was one of his nights for sleeping in the claw-foot tub, so she was in the other room curled up under the elephant's overhang, nestled beside the bed with plugs in her ears made from shredded copies of his stories, meant to keep the croons of the birds at bay. She was used to the smell. With her last young man, their cat got sick and hid on top of the fridge to die, and it was there for six days before they found it. It stayed there for another two years until he wrapped it in newspaper and put it in a box labelled *Kitchen Stuff*. The slow progression of the smell of death was something she'd grown accustomed to, but he, he had never been in love like this before, and so the smell reviled him. But the sound of the birds brought attention to the elephant on the bed, a bed which at one time had taken dominion over the apartment. She hated how the birds talked of nothing else. And every morning, after she left, the young man would come to the door, still always naked despite the cold, and he would stand on that small section of cleared floor and stare at the elephant, its trunk stuffed with maggots, its ass puckered with rot, its last defecation a dry, wide pie like a track of cooled lava fingering along the floor toward him. Every day after she left, he would stand there, staring, waiting for the elephant to breathe.

three

Before the elephant, they'd begun to sleep with a little space between them. That space was a no man's land where an elephant might go to germinate. It began as an ermine-sized space, but when the ermine clawed them up, the space got red fox wide. They didn't talk about it. She started hanging a foot off the edge, and he got comfortable with a naked arm on the cool wall. Neither tidied the sheets on the spot between them, which went up from sockeye salmon to capybara all the way—in a matter of weeks—to adolescent saltwater crocodile. Neither one's hand would wriggle there, even in their sleep. It was as if there was a ward cast on it. They didn't talk about it or across it, and the more they didn't, the more it grew. Once, on his side of the bed in the middle of the night, he mumbled "Marco" to her silence. Another night, after coming home late, the young man already in bed with both bare buttocks squished onto the wall, she slipped under her end of the covers, hung one full leg off the side, and whispered, "Leave room for God" to no responding chuckle. Just as the space between them was negotiated by their individual ignorances, its size was measured on separate scales. The placeholders were mere ideas of the size of the emptiness, and although they had similar ones, they didn't share any. Whereas he had an ermine, she had a weasel. Whereas she thought capybara, he thought beaver. Where he had a sockeye, she had a chinook, and her adolescent croc was the same as his morphed idea of an alligator. It wasn't until weeks of reassigning the widening gap into different phyla and genera that they both independently thought: elephant. There wasn't nearly that much room between them at the time, of course, but they both began to believe that their gap could be enough ground for a grey, trunked seedling. That the fetus of an elephant could fit there, grow out into a full calf that might bulge into adulthood. They thought this same thought as she was teetering over the edge of her side of the bed, and while he was fully pressed flat against his cold wall, with nothing but his left hand relaxing on the sheets. It was then that the energy of their distance began to shock and shudder forth the abstract thing they'd been ignoring concretely, but which before had simply been neurons mirroring like butterfly wings in their brains. It wasn't until the night when his hand finally tensed up to his body and she finally lost her centre and slipped off the bed that the elephant arrived, full adult and dying, because so long had they felt its presence, a negative presence in both its lack and affect, that by the time it arrived, it was sick. When the elephant arrived it had very little energy left, but with its last bits, it sat up on the bed, and with its trunk, peeled the young man from the wall—where he surely would have been pinned and suffocated by the elephant's weight—and dropped him softly on the floor beside the door. Then the elephant picked up the young woman from where she'd fallen off the edge of the bed—where she might have been susceptible to being splashed by any of the expulsions that might happen during the elephant's death—and placed her kindly beside the stove. Then the elephant, exhausted, lay back down on the bed to finally finish dying.

four

They had almost forgotten about the dead elephant when they finally snapped. She came back from work one day and found the window screen broken through and all the birds, the magpies, the crows, the ravens—or just bigger crows—and the buzzards picking at the corpse. He was trying, with the broom they never used, to swat them away from their food, edging back and forth around the corpse, throwing printed copies of his manuscripts at a bald eagle perched atop the bookcase on the far side of the elephant, just inches beyond the broom's reach. When she came in to this scene she said that she was through with the elephant, she couldn't handle it, they had to get rid of it. He paused, looking over at her, his eyes watering because the clothespin had finally, after all those weeks, snapped off his crimped nose, and he was once again smelling through splinter-thin nostrils the elephant, the rot, their stale air. His eyes watered and he agreed, and so that day they went to thrift shops across the city, buying up all the long knives and stained bedsheets, which they carried back up to the tiny second-floor apartment, where she held the door for him and he sharpened the knives for her, and together they cut large chunks of bad flesh off the flanks, the rump, the throat, and carried each piece down to the curb on a stretcher made of bedsheets bound between the broom and the coat rack. He saved her the trouble of the guts, and she saved him from having to pull the big eyes from the sockets. He wrapped its heart in one of its lopped-off, floppy ears, as she kited the mast of skin by running down the stairs, gripping onto the still-attached tail. Soon, there was nothing but bone on the bloody bed. So they broke the skeleton into bits and threw most of the smaller bones, the ribs, the vertebrae, the shins, out the hole in the window screen. The last part of the elephant they removed was the skull, which she rolled down the stairs alone, and by the time she made it back upstairs, wiping smeared maggot on her bloody dress, he'd already turned the bed on its side, and she helped him carry it down to the curb, just as he helped her throw the books and the coffee maker and all the spoons out the window, just as she propped the door open while he chucked each of her shoes down the stairwell, and just as he held her hand while she threw his previously unreachable underwear into the dumpster outside, until finally the apartment was barren, and they sprawled out on the blank floor together, until finally, hours, days, weeks later, she slung him over her shoulder, carried him down to the street, and watched each of the birds return, slowly, quietly dodging the first flakes of falling snow as they once had his pages, to carry him away into the whitening sky. By the time she made it back up to the apartment, alone, it was full winter, and the door, the door that she had once left open, was closed, and locked.

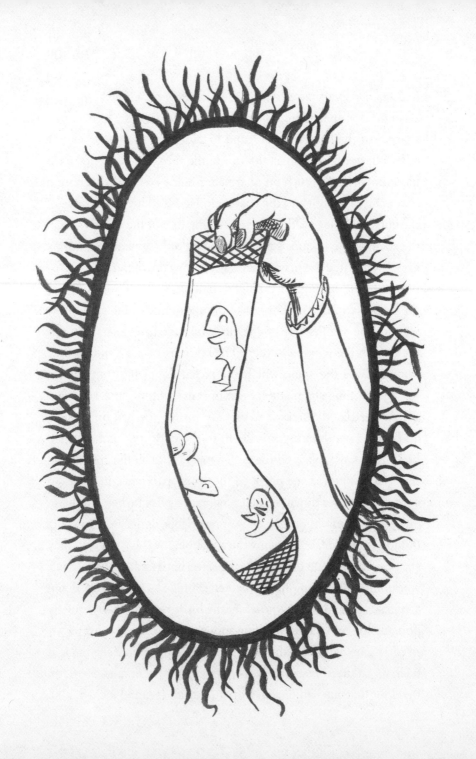

BLUENESS

THE NIGHT WHEN I WAS IN THE BATHROOM and heard a noise moving heavily through my apartment, I couldn't lock the door because there wasn't a lock.

Ted, the landlord, had the lock removed after his teenage daughter cut her wrists in the tub two days before her junior prom. She hadn't done that in my apartment in the third-floor attic, or in any of the apartments Ted leased out in Old Hyde Park, but in his family's house in Fairway. Ted didn't tell me anything about that. He just walked me through the apartment, the same apartment I'd stared at photos of on my phone in the days leading up to my arriving in Kansas City. At the bathroom all he did was close the door, open it again, and then say, "No locks."

Ted's brother, Carl—who did handy work in Ted's apartments— told me the story a week after I'd moved in, when he came to check the pipes because the bathroom sink suddenly started running at one-third pressure.

"They'd heard her whimpering on the other side of the locked door, and after he broke through with a crowbar he found her sitting in the tub, one cut in." As he sat there on his knees beside the toilet in my bathroom, Carl mimed it with the pipe wrench—cutting in the wrong direction to die. Ted had removed all the bathroom locks after that—in all the apartments he leased—on principle. "Cost him over $2,000 to remove them all," Carl said, pointing at the old door, at its glass knob and the gutless bolt turner underneath it. "Vintage." Then Carl took out a set of pliers from his pocket and unscrewed the trap from the tip of the faucet, and a big black blob blasted out. Shrugging, Carl stood up, looked down at the mass under the rushing faucet, and thumbed it through the drain cover.

So that night with the noise—two weeks after Carl fixed the water pressure—I couldn't lock the bathroom door. I could do nothing but sit there, listening, frozen, hoping that sitting blocked up on the toilet would not be where I died. Or worse.

———

I'd found the apartment on Craigslist one afternoon while waiting for the PATH train at Journal Square to 33rd Street in Midtown Manhattan. The PATH never came. A New Jersey Transit train had crashed into the train station in Hoboken, which was above the Hoboken PATH station, so all the trains were cancelled. Nobody had told me, so I stood there, browsing through apartment listings in Kansas City, when I saw this place: $600, one bedroom, shared washer and dryer in basement, all utilities included.

This had been a part of my commute ritual for the previous year or so, keeping an eye on apartments in cheap Midwestern cities, particularly Milwaukee, Detroit, St. Paul, and Kansas City. I would look until I walked onto the train, until my phone's connection died in the tunnel, then I would put my phone away and stare through my reflection in the door's window. But that afternoon the train never came, and by the time the Port Authority worker tapped me on the shoulder and told me that no train was coming, I'd flipped through all the photos of the attic apartment, with its obtuse and unfriendly for-hanging-things walls, and had emailed Ted. By the time I surfaced into street noise outside the station, he'd already emailed me back to say I could see it Sunday. In three days.

After I left the station, I walked over and rented a small U-Haul van, parked it on the other side of the street from my apartment, and slowly oozed all my things into it. My three roommates had each been able to get to their jobs. I was the only one who needed to use the train; everyone else worked loveless retail and food service jobs in our quickly whitening neighbourhood. I didn't leave a note. I wanted my roommates to realize by my absence how much I'd been contributing to the upkeep of our two-bedroom, wondered how long it would take them to notice I was gone, wondered if they might think for a moment that I'd died when that train hit the station. I kept my key. I left nothing but my mattress behind my closed bedroom door—the one thing in my life I couldn't bear alone.

When I left the bathroom after hearing the noise that night, I held my nail scissors like a movie murderer holds his knife. I moved like a shadow. I barked, "WHO'S THERE?" Nobody said anything. I didn't see anyone.

I checked the door to the apartment, and it was still chained and deadbolted. All the windows were shut and locked. The only strange thing I noticed was that the fridge door was open. All the aging leftovers inside the fridge that had gone bad and were waiting for garbage day had disappeared, but their containers were still there. Softly opened, as if they had cleanly breathed their contents out. But nothing was in the apartment except me and a fading smell of mildew.

—

I worked at a non-profit tech company focused on helping public school teachers get the materials they needed to better their instruction, on a team involved with slapping users' wrists. The company had a very positive attitude, a very start-up vibe—with team-defining acronyms and everything—despite being more than ten years old.

Everyone was all about love, about being open and liberally supportive, about helping make the world better by helping our country's teachers. I didn't speak up much; I mostly sat in a quiet corner and emailed or called people and told them they were no longer allowed to use our site because they were misusing it. I called them to ask what they were doing with the things they had gotten from the site. I called to tell them they had to return them. That their school had the right to call the cops on them if they didn't. My voice was calm, soft, and inflected upward, but it was still threatening. I'd honed that voice. Once, a colleague looked up at me after I got off a call and told me, with a smile—everyone there said everything with a smile—"You're such a *shrill!*"

I wasn't a shrill. I'd just learned how to make people do what I wanted them to do. I'd found the tone to make them listen. But I didn't really take pride in that. I removed from the site teachers who weren't in eligible schools, or who weren't working enough, or in the right way. I wagged my finger at them. I banned some. I removed whole schools. But I never liked having to do it.

On the day I'd left New Jersey, as the gas attendant was fuelling up the U-Haul just outside of Newark, I'd messaged my manager on Slack and told them I wasn't going to be back in the office for a while. That my mother, who lived in Kansas City, was sick, and I had to go and help her. My mother wasn't anywhere near there— she was in Elizabeth—but nobody had ever asked before, and as I was driving through the hills of Pennsylvania, my manager messaged me back:

> *No worries, Margarita! Sorry to hear about your mom* 😢
> *You can work remotely as long as you need.*
> *Oh, and I'm glad you weren't in the Hoboken station when that train hit it today!*
> *Ugh, so scary.*
> *Let me know what hours are good for next week as soon as you know, okay?*
> ♥

 I messaged back some smiley, positive words—thanking her, telling her I'd keep her in the loop—when I stopped for gas again in my brief pass through West Virginia. I think I'd been hoping, somewhat, that they'd just fire me. When I got to Columbus, I found a twenty-four-hour Walmart and slept in the van, sprawled out in the extra space in the back, the Leatherman multi-tool my father gave me open to the knife and sitting beside the U-Haul's keys, within easy reach. My body taking up the space where the stuff of a life should have been. In the morning, Saturday, I woke up and drove the rest of the way.

After work the next day, the day after I'd heard the movement in the apartment, I took a Lyft to Target and bought three aluminum baseball bats. I put one in my bathroom, one in my bedroom, and another in the living room. I made sure they were hidden so that I would be the only one who knew where they were in the case of a break-in.

I'd thought about taking another Lyft to a Bass Pro—or some other shop—and buying a gun instead. I knew you could do that in Missouri, but as soon as I started to fall for the idea, I saw a flash of me being randomly stopped in the street by a bored white police officer on my way home, of being asked to show them what was in the plastic bag, of me pulling out a pistol, and of me getting shot dead in the street. So I did not buy a gun.

After my leftovers were raided from the fridge that night, I'd started to think that maybe a raccoon was living in the building. Aside from the door, there was only one other way into the apartment, which was the laundry chute that led to the steamy, damp basement. I never bothered to lock the latch when I closed the chute, and it was large enough, I thought, for a raccoon to crawl through.

It was the only thing that made sense. I thought about asking the downstairs neighbours if they'd ever had anything strange like that happen, but I'd never said a word to them during the many times we'd crossed paths on the stairs. I imagined the raccoon lounging in my underwear, licking from its lips the gone-bad leftovers that I'd been keeping in the fridge until garbage day. I brought out the baseball bat from behind the window curtain in the living room and walked down to the basement. My downstairs neighbour was unlocking her door. I wondered if she'd heard me yelling at no one the previous night. I didn't say anything to her.

In the basement, I flipped the switch under the sign that said *Please turn the light off when you leave. —Ted* and held the bat in both hands. There was a distinct wet mildew smell down there that sometimes swelled up through the chutes and snuck into the apartment. There was a drain in the floor and all sorts of pipes webbing along the unfinished ceiling. I sniffed, looked around for evidence of life.

As closely as I looked, all I could find was mould. Mould fogging the little windows near the ceiling, mould in the cracks around the drain in the cement floor, mould crawling up the faucet of the slop sink. Under my chute, I threw my laundry basket of clothes onto the cement floor. Held the bat over my head. But there was no raccoon in there. There was nothing, nothing alive. I put down the bat and put all my dirty clothes back into the basket and went upstairs.

—

Transitioning from working in the Midtown office to working remote was easier than I'd thought, because there was something about it that felt honest.

I'd been working at the company for nearly two years, since I finished school at Kean University and moved out of my father's house to live in Jersey City. I'd studied education and history, but didn't end up getting my teaching certification. I did a practicum one semester, in a Title 1 school in Bayonne, teaching US history to sixth graders who called me Miss Veron. Two weeks before holiday break—the end of my time there—as I was mapping out the path of Lewis and Clark's expedition across the country on a roughly drawn-out America on the blackboard, one of my problem students chucked a rock wrapped in paper at the back of my head. I woke up in the nurse's office, half-blinded, and had to stay awake for twenty-four hours in the hospital while being monitored. I never went back to the practicum. So when I graduated, a semester late to give me time to recover from the concussion, I didn't do what I needed to get that certification. I didn't think I wanted to teach anymore. It wasn't so much the rock but the experience of standing apart from a bunch of people who were looking up at me while I told them what was what. What they should believe and know. Instead, I moved to Jersey City and ended up finding that job in Manhattan.

What felt honest about the transition to working remote was that I'd never really felt like I fit in there. I was the only person on the customer relations team who lived in New Jersey, and most everyone else—who lived in Brooklyn or Queens or Washington Heights—spent a lot of time hanging out together outside of work. Going to plays, going to bars, having house parties. I would have gone out, but nobody really tried that hard to get me to. I was always a little shy, and because nobody put the work into breaking through that, I never became the peg that fit. I just came to work, did my work, and hopped onto a packed PATH train back to my apartment.

As soon as I was working remotely in Kansas City, I felt properly removed, but it also felt like nothing had changed. It felt like I'd been working remotely for years, even though I had been at the same table as all of them, even though I'd sat beside them at our all-hands meetings, even though I'd laughed at their jokes and was in all their fun Slack channels.

Sitting on a blow-up mattress I'd bought at the Walmart in Columbus, wearing nothing but a pair of boxers from my last boyfriend and working with my laptop on my bare legs felt the same. I ordered in and barely left the house, mostly because I'd yet to get a car. I showered and dressed only on the days I had meetings with my manager, who would ask me about my mother. Every time she asked me, I was surprised. But making something up was always easy.

"It's so hard." I said. "She feels so far from me."

———

I didn't hear anything else moving around the apartment for the rest of that week or the next. I'd been sure to lock the door to the chute. I did better with eating my leftovers before they could go bad. After I took the trash out to the curb on Monday morning, I went downstairs again to wash the clothes I'd thrown onto the dirty cement floor. By then, my hamper was overflowing. When I opened the washing machine, I was hit by a big mildew smell and realized that my neighbour had left her clothes in there. A barely damp tangle of patterned panties and skirts and blouses. I didn't have enough quarters to both dry my clothes and rewash and dry hers, so I left them out on the little plastic table. They added to the wet, living smell of the basement. I punched my own clothes in.

Sitting atop the washing machine, scrolling through Instagram on my phone, I realized it was Halloween. I didn't have a costume; I didn't have anywhere to go and be someone else. I went on Facebook, where I'd not posted anything since leaving Jersey City, and saw that I'd been invited to a few Halloween events by people I knew in New York and in Elizabeth. There were also unread messages from my old roommates. They were probably cursing me. Or wondering if I was dead. I saw my mom posting about the election, all-caps and bad grammar, and I closed the app.

When the washer beeped and unlocked, I stuffed my wet clothes into the dryer and went back upstairs to get my computer. I wanted to work down there, in the wet, dim place. There was something about being down there that I liked. And I'd always loved getting into the rhythms of the dryer, sitting atop it while it tumbled, hot under me.

On the way back down, laptop under my arm, my downstairs neighbour was leaving her apartment again. I didn't say anything until I'd gone down the stairs and then I remembered the clothes. I thought to myself, "This is how you can break the ice," and so I turned around.

"Oh hi, you forgot your clothes in the washer," I said. "They smell a little bad, you may want to rewash them."

"Oh shit!" she said. "Sorry, god yeah I was washing them *last weekend*. They were from a trip I took out to Omaha for my grandma's birthday. I'll grab them now and wash them later. Thanks for letting me know!"

I smiled at her and turned around. I heard her a few stairs behind me as we went into the basement. I opened my mouth a few times to say something, knowing how much easier it was to get myself to speak without looking at the person, but then I didn't say anything and closed my mouth again. While I opened the door to the basement and walked down the stairs, down into the smell, I was imagining a month later: me and her drinking in her apartment and laughing about the man who lived on the bottom floor and smoked pot on Thursday nights, and how she would be the start of my knowing people here. As I got to the bottom of the stairs, I looked over at the table. The clothes were gone.

"Wait," I said, pointing at the table. "They were just here!"

My neighbour went up to the table, looked under it, didn't see anything. All that was left on the table was a single sock with little dinosaurs on it.

"What the heck," I said, as she turned around to look at me. Her little dinosaur sock dangled from her fingers. I looked at the sock instead of her.

⸻

"I've been meaning to get down here," Ted had said, as he walked me down the stairs to the basement the day I showed up to Kansas City, after he'd shown me the apartment. "To scrub it down, bleach it." He walked over to the coin-op washer and dryer and patted their tops, a hollow sound filling the air.

I don't remember ever being afraid of the basement beyond going down there with the bat to see if I could find the raccoon I'd

been convinced was living down there. I wasn't afraid of the basement, but now when I remember Ted bringing me down there and
talking about bleaching it clean, there is so much fear. But I don't
think I was afraid at all back then, as I walked behind Ted, achy
from sleeping on the floor of the U-Haul for two nights in a row, the
second time in another twenty-four-hour Walmart parking lot in
Independence. I just walked behind him, my long, dark, dirty hair
trailing out behind me, politely smiling and holding my chequebook
and a pen. Trying not to appear too eager to take the place.

What I was thinking about, in that space where I now remember an overwhelming fear, was being back in Elizabeth, a little
kid dragged to the laundromat by my mother because I was too
little to be left alone at home, even though my father left me alone
whenever I stayed with him. I remembered sitting on a chair
and watching my mother push our clothes in the laundry carts,
watching other Latina women standing in half circles around the
tables, folding endless baskets of clothes and watching soaps on
the television. Everything in Spanish, everything in that language
I'd never been taught because my father hadn't wanted to be left
out, at least not until he moved out.

I was thinking about standing there, by the swirling washing
machines, watching my mother and the other women work and
chatter. They would lift their hands to the television in the corner
of the ceiling, yelling at it, laughing. I was thinking about all of that,
aging through all those moments in the laundromats in Elizabeth
and then Jersey City. I tried to make those feelings fit into that little
mouldy basement, but I couldn't. I did not feel excluded from its
darkness or grime, or the coldness of the three tin chutes over the
three laundry baskets—one of which was completely empty.

Once we made it out of the basement and Ted flipped off the light behind us, I turned to him and said, "And I can sign a lease today?" The relief I remember after we left that basement was not relief that belonged to me then.

———

On a Sunday afternoon a few days after the noise had cleared out my leftovers, I had walked down to Westport. I had the urge to eat surrounded by people. I wanted to change the pace, to expose myself. I ended up in an Irish pub that was packed with a sea of red. The Chiefs were playing the Saints. I sat on a stool at the bar—a stool that was probably free because it was about the only one that didn't have a good view of the game—and I ordered a beer and a burger. Chiefs were up 21 to 7.

I asked the bartender for the burger medium-well with no tomatoes, and after she gave me the list of cheese options, I chose blue cheese. Maytag. I'd never had blue cheese before, and I wanted to try something new. I wanted to feel alive and different.

The people surrounding me didn't acknowledge me. I was wearing a gold blouse with white denim jeans. I felt excruciatingly small by the time my burger came, and I ate half of it—desperate for the gross newness of the cheese to my palate, having opened the burger to stare at the little pockets of blue in the crumble— before I couldn't stand being there anymore. So I got a box and took the burger home and sat on the air mattress, Netflix playing on the laptop set on the floor in front of me, breathing into my knees until I got up to go to the bathroom to wash my face, resolving to never try anything new again. It was only then, in the mirror, that I realized I was wearing Saints colours. I turned on the water, and after a few seconds of heating up, the water suddenly ran low again. So I went into the other room and got the Leatherman and used the pliers to take off the trap on the tip of the faucet, like Ted's brother Carl had. Out blasted another little black blob onto the drain cover, the size of a penny. My skin crawled.

I left the bathroom to get my phone. I wanted to take a picture of it, to google it and see what might be happening in the pipes. Something dying, perhaps, something that I was afraid could be poisoning me. As I stooped down to pick up my phone, I went light-headed for a moment and smelled the mildew smell of the basement in the room with me. The chute was still closed, still locked. I caught my breath, opened my camera app, and went to the sink. The black clot was gone. The drain cover clean, spotless.

I put my phone down. I put the trap back on the faucet and then went to the other room, sat down on the bed, and started to eat the rest of the burger and stare at my computer.

Something, though, did not taste right. By which I mean that it did not taste as it had before. I took off the bun to look, and the cheese was a crumble of half-melted white, entirely missing its off-tasting blueness.

———

When my neighbour left, she said she would ask Matt if he had come down and picked up her clothes. Matt was apparently the name of the guy who lived below both of us, on the first floor. I'd never talked to him either. She said goodbye before she left, and I stood there, hearing the dryer tumble, hearing zippers softly scraping inside, feeling stupid.

I climbed up onto the dryer and opened my laptop, and by the time I looked up from my computer, six hours had passed. My ass hurt from sitting there, and the battery of my laptop was on its last jolts. I'd worked, presumably, though I didn't remember it. I didn't really remember anything. I just climbed off of the dryer.

I can say this now, but I felt it when I was in the laundry room too: despite not having found proof of anything larger than a mouse living down there among the dirty clothes and the cluttered shelves and the piles of degrading building supplies, I didn't feel alone down there. I felt like there were many things watching me. I felt like there were many things trying to get my attention, trying to say things to me, only I wasn't in tune enough to hear them.

———

I'd always felt a little like I was teetering along a fringe. There were always circles that I was not part of. There were men who came into my life whom other women—who knew what they were— didn't warn me about. In school, I hit all my growth spurts first and experienced everything else last. I didn't know how to have sex until I'd done it for the second time, when I was twenty. I didn't know I could *enjoy* sex until I was twenty-three. Nobody had told me.

The thing I noticed about history in college is that when you look back at it, everyone is in one group or another. Thinkers who never met one another make up an intellectual movement, clusters of contested land make up empires, little events pile up like plot points in a linear story. Everything in history makes up history. I enjoyed that, how there were boxes for everything, and how no box only had just one thing. I wanted to experience that. I wanted to be in a very full box. I wanted to feel like a living, breathing part of something large. Because I never had.

But I was scared that I would be left alone, which meant that I would never fit into history. I'd felt like I never completely fit in one place enough, had never been part of a sizable unit, a collective. One of the closest experiences I'd ever felt was when a middle-aged white lady who got on the PATH to 33rd Street at Newport kept glancing at me until she walked over and grasped the bar beside my seat and asked me if I was Penélope Cruz. I shook my head and smiled, and she apologized to me, again and again, for the rest of the ride. It is sad, it is embarrassing, how good it felt to be misinterpreted like that. To be mistaken for a person of note.

—

After I brought up my laundry, I ate the leftover lo mein in the fridge from the previous night and put on clean clothes and walked to 7-Eleven. It was about 80 degrees, despite the fact that the next day was November, and I sweated through my newly cleaned clothes on the walk back, a six-pack of beer under each arm, bags of snacks dangling from my fingers. By the time I made it back to my apartment, the sun was going down, and kids were already out in their costumes. They went from door to door in their little flocks, pillowcases and plastic jack-o'-lantern buckets in their hands, parents walking behind or waiting at the sidewalk or absent. Superheroes, princesses, ghosts. I watched as a group of little kids went up to our house's door and waited. I slowed down. None of my neighbours came to the door. By the time they turned around to leave, I was walking across the lawn. The kids turned to me, but their parents saw the beers under each arm and urged them next door. I didn't mind. I hadn't bought anything to share. I went inside.

The man I now knew was named Matt was playing music in his apartment, and the door was half-open. He was standing there, dressed as Batman but without his cowl on, taking a shot. There was a girl dressed as Harley Quinn, and another as Hillary Clinton, hanging off the arm of someone in a loose blue suit and a Trump mask. I walked up the stairs without stopping. When I got inside, I locked the door and opened a beer.

By then, it'd gotten to the point that I never felt more like myself than when I was not participating in something. So I didn't really mind too much, hearing the sounds of their fun bounce around. I opened the laundry chute and heard it resonate up to me. I pulled a chair up beside the chute and listened to them pregame before going out to a party. I eventually heard the voice of the girl who lived beneath me. "Sara!" Matt called exuberantly. "What are you supposed to be?"

"Pocahontas! Obviously."

They laughed, and I went to the fridge and got another beer.

"Why would I have taken your laundry?" Matt asked.

"I didn't think you did, but it's gone. Do you think she took it? That'd be weird if she took it and told me about it."

"I mean, she seems weird. Maybe she's into mind games."

I closed the chute. I finished the beer. I got another beer, and the sounds were gone. I was alone in the house. I felt snapped off and very lonely and tipsy. I got out my phone and scrolled Instagram. I felt lonely, but I somehow didn't feel alone. I opened the chute again and stuck my head inside. I breathed the silence in deep, the soft mildew smell slowly rising from the basement.

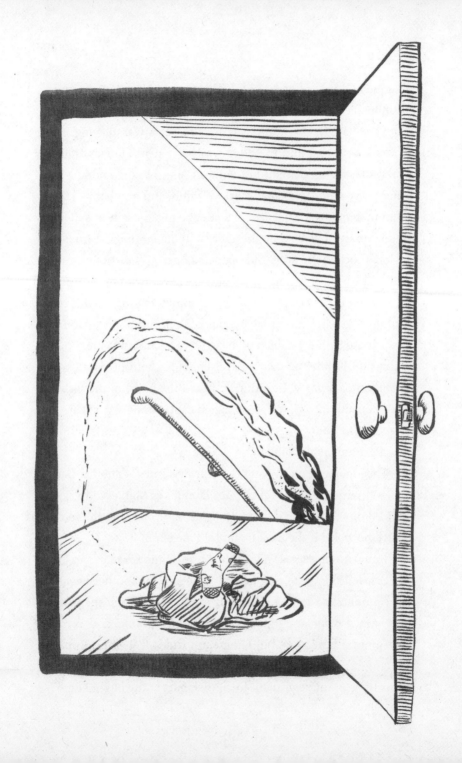

Then there was a knock at my door. It was soft and slightly metallic, and I pulled my head from the chute and tiptoed toward the door to listen closer as it came again. I imagined some small kid had wandered up the stairs, getting in as the neighbours left.

As I got closer to the door, the mildew smell grew stronger and stronger, and so when I opened the door I thought I knew what I would find: the clothes, somehow. Which I did. But holding the clothes clumped together, using the clothes to make a human-esque form, was a deep and wriggling and fuzzy blackness. I stared at it. I thought to hold my nose, but I didn't. I breathed it in. Where a face would be, there was the mate to my neighbour's dinosaur sock. I later realized that this sock had been chosen because it was something I was sure to recognize. It raised the hand it had knocked with—a hand made up of bundled-up jean shorts, with the metal buttons of the fly pointing out like knuckles. It unfurled the shorts as though to wave, then all of my neighbour's clothes began to fall, like pieces of flesh. The last to fall was the sock, and when it did, the whole creature fell apart. Slowly, it dissipated in a receding gradient along the walls, down the stairs, until it had spread itself so thin I could not tell if it was still there or if it had left.

Trick or treat, I might have thought, crouching down to my neighbour's clothes. I took them in my arms, thinking I would clean and dry them and fold them and leave them outside her door—to make her feel bad for the way she thought of me—but they were dry, and they no longer smelled of mildew. They didn't smell like anything. Not detergent, just fresh. I took them downstairs and dropped them unceremoniously against her green wooden door.

I know I should have been surprised when I opened the door to a clutch of mould pretending to be a human, constructing its shape by making bones of my neighbour's clothes, but I wasn't. Or maybe I was, at the time, and I am misremembering. So much has changed; so many of the intense feelings I must have had throughout my life have smoothed out. It doesn't feel like it matters to remember the emotions anymore, so I don't. The facts of my life are still there, and one can assume from the events I lived through that I felt intensely about them, but it turns out that all those emotions we bottle up and lock up in ourselves—to torture ourselves—are held up in the insignificant gaps between the bits that are the *most* us. Which means that when your being breaks down—*transcends*—these feelings are the first things to fall through the cracks. So when I opened my mouth the next day, the feelings never had a chance. It wasn't so much a feeling of weight being lifted from me; it wasn't relief so much as a sense that the weight was not, and had never been, a real part of me.

—

I slept a fitful, dreamless sleep. Maybe there were dreams, but they either left me minutes after waking, as they usually did, or they would be gone soon. Along with much else. I didn't shower. I turned the AC off and opened the windows to the rising and unseasonably warm November day. I opened the laundry chute. I was still wearing the clothes I'd sweated through. I'd slept in them. My head felt too small for my brain. I didn't change.

A fog covers parts of that day, because my mind never got the opportunity to relentlessly dwell on it, never got to drown it in the tar pits of memory. In looking back, there was hunger in the apartment with me. Hunger that wasn't mine but would become mine, and my own different hunger. In looking back, my own hunger, which was to be forgiven the torment of my body, mixed with the apartment's hunger for there to be less in the world that was not part of it. That hunger was so loud and wide that I wonder if I felt it then. If it had crossed over to me. Looking back now at that morning in the apartment, that hunger is so loud that it is hard for me to remember what it was like to be in that lone, little body.

What I do know is that the image of the creature built of laundry standing outside my door, dropping its body into a pile of clothes while dissolving away, was playing and replaying through my head. That it had been replaying since I opened the door to it. I kept seeing its dinosaur-sock face. Which felt like the warmest, most welcoming face I'd ever seen.

What I do know is that I googled "cheese stores in KC," called a Lyft to take me to the Plaza, and left the apartment. My mind was vignetting, tunnelling in. As I left, I thought only of the creature. I felt a part of them in my body, having breathed them in while in the laundry room. I felt I'd been breathing them in, in one way or another, my whole life. As I was going down the last flight of stairs to the door, I heard a door open and close on the floor above me. My neighbour's feet—Sara—climbing down after me quickly, as if trying to catch up. When I went out the door, I did not hold it open. I let it close.

"Hey, hey!" she was saying, while I walked across the dewy lawn to the sidewalk. My Lyft was still seven minutes away. "Hey! Hey!"

I didn't turn around. I didn't make it seem as if I'd heard her.

"I'm sorry if I was weird about the clothes," she said. "Thanks for finding and cleaning them for me.

"You did, right? Matt said he didn't, and I'm sorry, really.

"Hey.

"Are you okay? You don't look so good. Are you sick?

"I'm sorry, I didn't mean it like that. Really.

"Do you want to talk? Do you want to have drinks later? I have to go to work.

"I'm sorry about the laundry, but you're being really rude.

"Hey.

"*Hey.*

"Matt was right."

The Lyft came, I climbed in, and the man turned around and asked me, "Going to the Plaza?"

My mind had become a pin. "I'm buying cheese." He said some other things, but I don't remember. I didn't respond. I was grieving all the fading leftovers I'd thrown out the day before with the trash. The driver turned on some music eventually, and then he dropped me off. I said nothing. As I left, I tipped three dollars.

I walked into the store, the Better Cheddar. I went to the register and asked, "Where are your blue cheeses?" They showed me. They said some things that I didn't retain, but as they brought me to the section, I asked, "And the blue is *mould*, right?"

"Yes, but it's totally safe. Do you need any help picking something out specifically?"

"I have $1,847 in my bank account. If I can get all of this for that, I'll take all of it. If not, I'd like $1,847 worth."

"Excuse me?"

I didn't think explaining my reasons would matter, but I did anyway. "I was saving up for a car. But I want this instead."

The next thing I remember is eating as much of the stinky cheese as I could without throwing up and then lying down, sweating and nauseous on the sweaty floor of my apartment with roquefort and Danish blue and Gorgonzola and Cambozola and—of course—Maytag smeared on my face, my neck, stuffed in my pockets, held between my knees, and scattered in a circle around me. I had my mouth open, breathing hard toward the laundry chute. Hunks of the assortment of stinky cheese were strewn out in a line from my open mouth to it. Waiting.

—

Two people claimed to have seen God in me, as if they knew. The first was my mother. She said that when I opened my eyes to her the first time, in the hospital, she saw the whole of everything swirling through my dark eyes. It took her breath away, she said. She told me that story a lot, so many times that it stopped meaning anything.

The second person was Leon, the first person I had sex with. Back before I knew I was supposed to enjoy it. I was nineteen. He was twenty-two. We'd met at a party and I got drunk near him, and he came back to my dorm room. My roommate was with her family in Atlantic City. After he got done kissing me for a while he sat on the bed, and I took off my top. Just before I took off my skirt, he stopped me.

"Wait," he said, staring. "Just stay there, like this." He leaned forward, his face getting closer and closer to my breasts. I could feel his breath's inertia breaking softly against my flesh. "You are too beautiful. You've got God in you, so close to the skin." Then he lay back and opened his hand to me, as if he were hitting Play on a porn video. I took off my skirt. I didn't look him in the eye because I was drunk and because I knew that if I did, I wouldn't be able to stop laughing. Then, sex happened to me, ending as he said, "Oh wow." It was only a religious experience in that it felt like going to church. I was glad for it to be over.

I didn't know until one night a few years later—after I'd learned women could enjoy sex—that Leon had fucked some of my friends from my dorm as well, and that each had had the same experience. Down to the body language, the same. "He sees God in every tit," one of us said, and everyone laughed. "Maybe God being there was what made the sex so bad," I said.

My mom, Leon—everyone was wrong. God didn't exist in me, not yet, if you could even call this God. It's not that. It's something local, inhuman, disparate, and sentient. It is not one thing, but a whole network of things holding on to one another, letting each other go off alone until they come back and taking them in again. It's not God, but if there's a heaven, this is it.

———

And so, eventually, it came. Down the wall, from the chute, an incorporeal blackness spread. As it came, it didn't bother to try to appear human; it just slowly crawled along, pulling the blue from all the cheese into its ranks. Surrounding me, her—*Margarita*. Slipping into my pockets, caressing my neck, pressing like a pillow against my welcoming face. It did not feel like anything but breath as it came in, forking into my lungs, my blood, the cheese ball of my stomach.

And so, with my consent, I was broken down alive. We broke me down; I broke down into us. It took days. And as I became a fuzzy, fungal mass—feeding us and becoming us at once—I felt all the distance go away. All that pain, all that anger, sadness, trauma, love. And I sort of just became *beingness*, became so many parts that didn't need to add up into a whole. There was no such thing. I began to live for holding the filament of another little fungus. I became the blackness that moves invisible on air, that enthrones death, that feeds along the wet. I tumbled down the chute into the many-ness of this dark, rifled through the dirty clothes of my neighbours, slowly consumed any organic matter I could find. Consumed and converted.

I cannot properly relate this feeling, this transcendence, because feeling is nothing to me but a tone shuddering through the network. There is so much sound, as if the world were a radio tuned in to every station at once. I can pick up on the trees lining the street, talking to one another through the fungal network of the soil, can hear messages all through the city moving like light bouncing and never stopping. It is like I have a connection to a wideness. And I am wideness, or at least a collection of small participants in it.

What I am a part of now is everything. I do not begin anywhere and I do not end anywhere. Sometimes I can come together, sometimes the messages add up to make up what approximates who I was before. Like now. But most of the time, I am simply unidentifiably within. I am here. I am there. I am not, while I also still am. And when I don't feel like I want to remember any of it, I simply crawl back into the absolution of the surge. I disperse for a time. I turn my world off and become the rest of the world.

And the feeling that I have for every single little aspect of us, as we cradle and reincarnate the dead into our network, as we encroach to try and cleanse and persist and widen—the feeling is indescribable. There is nothing in that world like it. Nothing that I knew, at least, or nothing that came here with me.

It is, I think, a feeling you might call *peace*. Or *home*.

ENGAGEMENT

WHEN I COULDN'T GO ON SOCIAL MEDIA without getting sad or angry, I hired an intern. A quiet kid from one of my first-year composition classes. After the second week of class, as I was erasing notes from the whiteboard about how to paraphrase without plagiarizing and the students were getting up to leave, I asked, "Is anyone interested in an internship opportunity?" By the time I turned around, the class was empty except for him, smiling.

At first, the intern came up to the shared adjunct office, and I told him about how I wanted him to run my social media because I was "too busy" writing my books and teaching. I didn't tell him how being on Twitter and Instagram had started to feel like volunteering to be flayed, like I was slowly transforming into nothing but empty skin blowing in the wind. I told him to study up on my posts for a week and then come back and I'd quiz him. The next week, after class, he came up to my office and told me what I would tweet if I were walking my dog and someone—as often happened—asked me what breed of terrier he was, and I had to tell them I didn't know. He offered a few different options for humorous observations I might make about how weird it is that it's acceptable to question an animal's ethnicity, or about how I was going to start making up random terrier breeds to answer that question. I offered him three photographs—a photograph of my dog panting beside me imitating him, a screenshot of an announcement about a poetry chapbook I had coming out, and another of my new-old bicycle—and asked him to caption them in my voice. I sat there for four minutes while he wrote captions and then handed them to me. Once he was done, I took his phone and logged him in to each of my accounts. After he left, I went on my phone and logged myself out.

I felt better, though he then started to email me a few times a week to see if he could get any new photos or tidbits from my life that I might want to share online. Within the week, I sent him my address and told him to swing by. He came up, met my partner and our dog, and I told him, "Take pictures of whatever you think would be worth posting about. Stock up." He went around the apartment and took a picture of my coral cactus, my national writing award collecting dust among the clutter on my bookcase, and my dog crawling over my partner as she tried to do yoga after a run. When he asked again if I had any stories to share, I meditated on the flatline of my days and didn't know what to tell him, so I just opened my arms to the apartment and said: "Paraphrase."

By the end of the month, I handed him a key to the apartment. In the morning, he would come by and walk the dog to the park and back. My Twitter filled up with pictures of my dog being walked and little witticisms about him. He tricked my dog into posing for reaction GIFs by holding a tennis ball out of sight from the camera and slowly moving it. He got a lot of likes that way, and a lot of replies. Engagement. Eventually, after our class on revision, he asked me what he was to do with the messages he was getting, which were meant for me and seemed personal. I sat back in my creaking chair, thinking, and eventually I said, "Write back to them. I don't want them to think I don't like them."

After he started having heart-to-hearts with my friends and fans, he reached out and told me he wanted to better represent me and my writing online, so I emailed him copies of the books I'd finished and the ones I'd been meaning to finish, now that I finally had so much time for writing. After he read the books, his tweets got better, started using the #amwriting hashtag to tease the content of the books in progress. As the tweets got better, it made sense to invite him to sleep on the couch and finish writing the books for me. I sat him down and told him where I thought they were heading, told him which were on submission and where. He began to sit at my laptop for hours on end, my headphones in his ears, my music coursing through them. Soon, every morning I had nothing to do but wake up and make coffee for him and my partner, though a week after he moved onto the couch, he started making the coffee too.

Eventually, I had to be honest with him. I told him he was doing a great job and that things were so much better with the extra time and headspace, but that I was starting to feel weird about his gender. He was cisgender, and it had started to seem uncomfortable to me that he was running a trans person's accounts and writing a trans person's books. When I told him that, he broke down and said, "No, no, no. I'm just like you." By the end of the week, his nails were bright red, and he was using gender-neutral pronouns too.

They were, I mean.

Eventually, my intern was sleeping in the bed with my partner, and I was sleeping on the couch with the dog—until the dog began climbing into bed with them. I slept in late, past their waking up and getting dressed and walking my dog and making coffee and kissing my partner goodbye and writing my books and, two days a week, riding my new-old bike to teach my classes. I was nothing but an adjunct, so nobody seemed to notice. Since I had so much more time on my hands, I started to follow them and sit in their old spot in the classroom, and a few weeks later they asked me to stay after class, and we went up to their shared office to talk. I sat across from them. They reached into their messenger bag and pulled a paper I'd written about augmented reality games out of a folder and slid it over to me. "I'm a little worried about your work," they said, tapping the emblazoned *D* on the top of the page. They told me to make sure I did the revision, because my grade would need it. I took the paper home with me, to the dorms, and I had my roommate read it over. He told me he agreed with my instructor's notes. He agreed with the grade.

Even if my grades were suffering, I felt so much lighter than I had in such a long time. I felt good when my instructor announced at the beginning of class that they'd just sold a novel on top of their recent poetry chapbook. The class clapped. I clapped along with everyone, emboldened to live in a world where a trans person could have the success they seemed to be having. I felt happy for them. I knew how hard they worked. After class, I went up to the front of the classroom and congratulated them, and they looked over at me, not making eye contact for long. "Thanks," they said. "Have a nice week."

It was sometime after Thanksgiving that they came in and showed off their new vintage blue-stoned ring. "Engaged!" they said, their hair-framed face flushing. We clapped again.

I felt so good and so happy for them, which made me wonder why I didn't feel very happy for myself, which made me look at my life and realize how much time I spent smoking pot with my roommate and watching anime late into the night when I should have been researching and writing and revising my papers. How I was going into debt to go to school without really knowing who would come out the other side to pay it off. How I had not been on a date in months, and nobody even seemed to look at me. How I hadn't ever really looked at myself either. I went on Twitter and saw people tweeting about how people like me—cisgender, straight white men—were destroying the world. I felt sad, and then I felt angry because I felt powerless. It all seemed so true.

At the end of the semester, as I put off my schoolwork, I was completely addicted to social media. I was online so much again, scrolling endlessly through Twitter and Instagram and TikTok, feeling bad about myself and still feeling sad. So much life I wasn't a part of. I felt thin and empty. I liked so many things, retweeted so many things, commented and shared. I was so engaged in everything and everyone, but nobody was engaged in me. I eventually found myself searching my instructor's social media and seeing what they were up to. I didn't follow them because they were my instructor, and I thought that would cross a line. They posted cute engagement photos of them and their partner and their dog.

They had a series of photos of them signing book contracts and announcing the recent receiving of arts grants. They had six times as many followers as they'd had months ago. People kept posting photos of their chapbook, kept saying how excited they were to preorder their forthcoming book of fiction. Everything seemed to be going so well for them. Everyone seemed to care.

Scrolling through their profiles in the dark, I was unable to shake the question. What had I done to deserve this life? Why did they get all of that attention instead of me?

On the last day of the semester, when I turned in my final essay for their class, which I had started writing three hours before it was due, they asked me if I'd done any of the revisions of my C and D papers. "No," I said. "I didn't have the time." They looked down at the paper, pulling a smile that was clearly out of politeness. Their lips were painted a bright shade of pink. Only the previous week, they had told the class that they were starting to use she/her/hers pronouns. "I see," they said to me. I mean, she said to me. "I hope you do better on this one."

After I failed the class, I spent the winter break online. I decided not to take my parents' money to fly back to Florida for Christmas, claiming I had a lot of work to do to make up for a difficult first semester, claiming I had to prepare to retake the composition class I'd failed since the class was required to graduate. But over break, while I was online, crashing on the couch in my roommate's family's basement far out in the suburbs, I wasn't preparing for that. Instead, I created a plethora of fake Twitter accounts and fake Instagram accounts and started messing with my former instructor. It started off small, posting emojis and GIFs that seemed inappropriate, considering what I was responding to.

Posts that I knew would confuse her. After she started blocking some of my accounts, I started tagging in anti-trans accounts to her tweets. It was a low blow, I knew, but I wanted to make her feel as inhuman and small as I felt. Once I started down that path, I committed. I woke up early, did some push-ups to turn my brain on, and started tweeting and commenting on her posts. Every time an account of mine got blocked or banned, I made two new ones, as if I were some kind of troll hydra. I started posting "guess whooooo??!?!!" from accounts created on new IP addresses when mine got banned. After a month of this, she started tweeting and posting on Instagram less. By then, she had already locked her accounts to new followers, but I'd prepared for that. Just before I started tagging in anti-trans accounts, I'd taken a few days to create forty or fifty real-seeming accounts that I followed her with before the real onslaught started. Sleeper cells I could awaken as needed. As time went on, her follower count stagnated, no longer steadily growing, and eventually she stopped posting altogether. I'd won, I thought. I was finally good at something, I thought.

A few weeks after she stopped posting, after I got a D on my first essay in my new composition class in the spring, I saw her leaving campus, and I followed her home. After I found out where she lived, I stopped the car and turned around. A week later, I went back. I didn't know what I was doing, not really, but I knew I was furious, and that she hadn't posted online in nearly a month. I felt so far away and pointless. The one thing I had excelled at had been taken away from me. After waiting around an hour or so, she came out of her apartment building, both her and the dog shuffling on the sidewalk in the slush-mud of February. As they walked down the street toward where I was parked, I stepped out and started yelling at her. Telling her that she wasn't all she was cracked up to be. That she was a bad teacher anyway. That her class was shit and that she clearly played favourites. That my failure was her failure. As I yelled, her dog hid behind her legs, and her face fumed in the cool air, her nails chipping in her fists. She looked exhausted in a way that made me so angry.

"You bitch!" I said to her, after I'd stopped yelling and she'd taken a few steps in my direction. "You ugly bitch!" I said, as she wrapped her arms around my body. "You hideous—" I said, as her skin opened up to a great rabid darkness inside of her, which I found myself both cursing and flinging myself into.

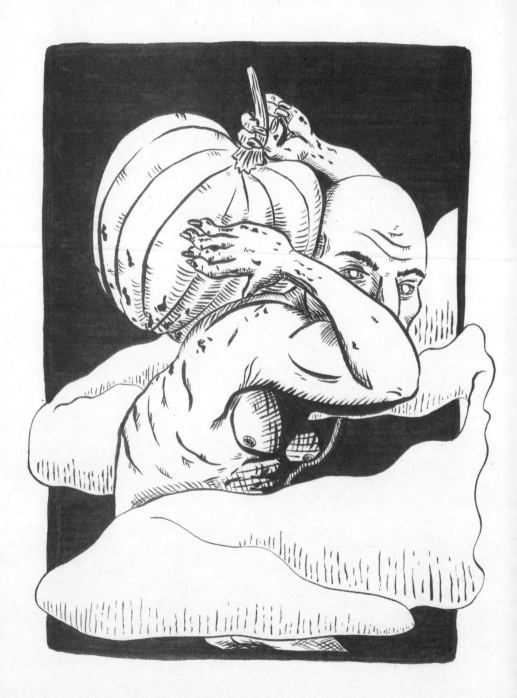

THE TROLL PATCH

ELSIE ENJOYED WATCHING THE TROLLS harvest the pumpkin patch. She'd go out in the mornings, when the pumpkins were plump and glistening with dew, and fix her eyes on the trolls' backs in the distance—taut and green like the promise of unripe tomatoes. Elsie enjoyed gallivanting through the fog to the near edge of the patch in the cool autumn air. Autumn was her favourite time of year, because she loved thick sweaters, hot chocolate, and these little green men, with their hunched backs and cleft chins. When she reached the prime age of seven, she figured that the trolls must hibernate through the rest of the year and come out of their hibernation only for the pumpkin harvest, because even though she lived on the farm with her daddy—except on weekends—she didn't start seeing the trolls in the fields until the pumpkins were ready to be picked, at the end of September, or sometimes the first of October.

Her daddy told her, ELSIE, REMEMBER, DON'T GO OUT
INTO THE PATCH. YOU CAN WATCH THE TROLLS FROM THE
EDGE—JUST DON'T GO OUT INTO THE PATCH. THE TROLLS
ARE VERY TERRITORIAL. THEY THINK THE PATCH IS THEIRS,
AND EVERYTHING THERE IS AN OBSTACLE TO THEM.

"But then why do *we* get the puntkins?" Elsie would say, and
had been saying every year, her pronunciations slowly progressing toward the accepted sounds of the words. At five she'd said,
"Why we get pun-kings?" Before that, at four, she'd simply thrown
a tantrum, lying on her back and flailing her limbs like a tipped
turtle because her parents—mostly her mommy—wouldn't let her
go visit the trolls after she'd first discovered them.

Puntkins was Elsie's invention at seven. At six she'd learned to
pronounce everything correctly, so she knew better than to say
"puntkins" now, but over the last year she'd developed a quietly
rebellious attitude that her daddy believed sprang from the divorce.
It was her mommy's doing, was what he meant. He believed
Mommy was teaching Elsie all the bad things she knew.

This year, when Elsie first said "puntkins," her daddy told her,
while slouching forward in his chair, drinking an Irish coffee, and
writing alimony cheques for his ex-wife—it was the last Friday of
September, and the trolls had recently begun the harvest—that the
trolls did not like the pumpkins. They actually hated pumpkins
being in their patch, and that was why they took the pumpkins
out and piled them up on the trucks. Once the pumpkins were
on the trucks, he drove them out to stores in the region where
people could buy them. Then, people either cut faces into them or
smothered them in pies.

In the years before, her daddy had given different excuses for why they got all the pumpkins the trolls harvested. When she was five, he said the trolls took the pumpkins off the patch because they were allergic to them. When she was six, the trolls were obsessed with the greenery of the patch matching the greenness of themselves, and the colour orange simply enraged them. In every version though, the trucks were the trolls' best solution for getting rid of the pumpkins. In every version, her daddy was always helping the trolls. And when Elsie asked, at seven, "Why do you put the puntkins on their patch when you know the trolls don't like them?" he looked up from his coffee and said, BECAUSE I BOUGHT THE LAND, FAIR AND SQUARE. THEY JUST DON'T BELIEVE IT'S MINE, SO THEY TAKE THE PUMPKINS OFF THE LAND. I'VE EVERY RIGHT TO SELL THEM. IT'S JUST A HAPPY COINCIDENCE IT WORKS OUT LIKE THAT. BESIDES, TROLLS ARE SO DARNED LAZY, IT'S GOOD TO GIVE THEM SOMETHING TO DO.

—

At the edge of the patch, seven-year-old Elsie watched the little green men yanking the "puntkins" from their stems, propping and piling them up on their strong backs, and carrying them to the trucks that her daddy had positioned along the roads that gridded the ten-acre patch. She watched them gently stack the pumpkins on the truck before hulking off for more beneath the thick ceiling of fog—a fog that was more a crawl space at that point, but that would dissolve into a ceiling, then into the sky itself as the sun rose. She thought they must have worked throughout the nights, because the trucks were always almost full by the time the light began to break in the morning, when Elsie would sneak out, swaddled in a big scratchy autumn sweater, to watch them. Without fail, they were always working at a distance from Elsie. She decided that they must start by first picking the pumpkins on the edges nearest to the farmhouse, in the deep dark of the fresh night, so that they would be closer to the forest when the sun finally rose. Often she wondered if they even saw her there, standing on the brink. And by the time the sun rose above the treeline—the fog not yet completely dissipated but a high, thin canopy—the trolls quietly disappeared into the dark trees where Elsie was never allowed to go. She was not allowed to go because, as her daddy said, the trolls lived in little foxholes, so if she went into their forest, she might fall into one and never return. He told her that trolls were very territorial.

Elsie thought those holes were poorly named. At school, two weeks before the harvest began, she wrote a story about a young troll who had a lot of trouble digging his foxhole until a young girl came and helped him. In her story, Elsie redubbed the foxhole a "trole." Her teacher, while appreciating the wordplay, couldn't help but say, "But what happens when you say that word out loud? It sounds the same as troll. That's called a homophone. So if you are listening to the story out loud, it sounds like your troll is having trouble digging himself, or his race. Also, aren't trolls very hairy? And don't they live in brambles, or in the mud under bridges?"

It was as if her teacher had never seen a troll, but what confused Elsie the most was why anyone might say the word out loud. A story was a silent thing. That was what her daddy said when he brought her books for bedtime stories and left them on her bedside table for her to read quietly to herself in the lamplight until she got too sleepy.

—

Elsie had only once seen a troll up close. She was four, and she had run away from the house because her mommy and daddy were fighting, and Elsie didn't like to listen to them fight, especially so early in the morning. They were very loud. So she ran downstairs, grabbed her bright-yellow galoshes and a thick brown sweater and the cookie jar full of her favourite monster cookies for sustenance and ran out of the house. As she closed the door, pressing her little weight into it perhaps too loudly, she heard her mommy begin to cry.

She was going to run into the woods. The forest seemed to be a place of silence. Back then, she'd never seen the trolls before, had no idea that trolls existed—at the farm or anywhere else. She was running into a darkness filled with things unimaginable to her. She had heard of trolls in stories but had always imagined them being tall, fat, hairy things that lived under bridges and tried to trick you into letting them eat you. They were loud and mean in the stories, and she believed that they only existed in lands far, far away.

When she reached the beginning of the patch and began slowly walking through the soggy soil, she noticed that the pump- kins were less numerous than the day before. They had almost completely disappeared from the edges of the patch. It was very foggy that day, and she couldn't see more than fifteen feet ahead of her. She kept walking, her cookie jar clamped in her tiny arms, wondering where all those pumpkins had gone and dreaming of Cinderella's coach, when suddenly she saw a figure of her height coming toward her through the fog. From the way it hunched over, its foggy shadow looked like it had no head. She froze, clasping the cookie jar close to her, as the figure came into her range of clear vision. It came up in front of her, staring at her galoshes, and gently picked her up, only to put her back down a few feet to the left. There had been a pumpkin behind her, huddling beneath huge, dry leaves. The figure reached down with callused green hands, which were not much bigger than her own but were pure strength, and plucked the pumpkin from the stem as if it were a fat grape on a weak vine.

Elsie didn't know what the thing before her was or what the safety protocols for the situation were. Out of fear, as when one faces a bear, she opened her ceramic cookie jar, pulled out one of the monster cookies, and held it out for the troll as he was turning back the way he'd come through the fog, the big pumpkin balanced in the crook of his neck. He stopped and looked at her, not saying anything, and then he opened his mouth. After a few seconds, Elsie walked forward, put the cookie in the troll's mouth, and stepped back. He walked on, disappearing into the fog, never once uttering a sound.

Then she heard her daddy raging his way out onto the lawn, heard him calling after her, trudging out in her direction. He followed her path through the long, dewy grass and along the line of her little imprints in the muddy soil. When he came through the fog, Elsie was scared, so scared that she dropped her mommy's cookie jar, and when her daddy found her, he told her she shouldn't run away like that. He grabbed her and slung her across the back of his neck, a historically playful gesture—though not playful then—grumbling as they went back to the house. Elsie didn't say anything about the cookie jar, but before it got out of sight, she saw a small congregation of slouching, seemingly identical trolls approach the jar, touch it, pick it up, then disappear back into the rising fog.

At the house, her mommy was crying on the stoop, staring at the ground, holding her gut. IT'S ALL YOUR FAULT, Daddy whispered to Elsie as they got closer. She smelled coffee and gross on his mouth. YOU MADE MOMMY CRY. ARE YOU PLEASED WITH YOURSELF?

—

But Elsie at seven, with her new rebel attitude, was resolved to see more of these pumpkin-picking trolls. She decided she wanted see them up close again before another harvest ended, and she was running out of time. On Friday morning before school, she woke up late, got dressed, grabbed her backpack, and walked out toward the patch with only enough time to glimpse the trolls as green-stippled drips in the equally green-blurred distance. It was getting closer and closer to when the trolls disappeared for the year. Elsie stood at the edge of the patch until she heard the door slamming and her daddy groggily grumbling down the steps toward his truck. ELSIE, IT'S TIME TO GO, COME ON.

After Mommy had left, Elsie had to switch over to a new school that was nearer to her mommy, otherwise she wouldn't have been able to get to her mommy's house on the days she stayed with her, which were mostly weekends. Which meant Daddy had to drive Elsie to school every morning. He would grumble, stop at a gas station on the way to pick up doughnuts and a huge coffee, and drop her off, just barely on time. Which meant she never got to sit around and talk with the other kids before school started, like she had done every morning at her old school. It kept her at a unique distance from everyone. On that Friday, her daddy dropped her off and patted her on the head after a quiet car ride, his eyes barely open, his mouth still asleep in a frown. She shuffled quickly to class.

In class, Mrs. Daryl talked about the Halloween party, which they would be having on October 28, another Friday because she didn't want to *start* the following week with a party. Meanwhile Elsie started composing a plan to meet the trolls that weekend. She titled it *Plan A for Action* in green coloured pencil. As Mrs. Daryl, in her cat-eye glasses and ankle-length floral dress, went down her aisle, asking everyone what he or she was bringing to the party, Elsie wrote down her options for the plan:

1. Sneak out at night.
   - Pros: Daddy probably asleep, more time to find trolls.
   - Cons: Spooky/dark, Daddy may not be asleep, Me tired.

2. Tell Mommy I want to stay weekend at Daddy's for Harvest Festivities but then sneak off when she takes me home.
   - Pros: Daddy might not see me come home and won't know I'm there and not at Mommy's, so can sneak out earlier.
   - Cons: Daddy might notice so need to make Plan B (for Backup).

Before Elsie could add a third option to the list, she noticed Mrs. Daryl finishing up with the boy ahead of her—James, who always had a bag lunch filled with mixed greenery, for which he was called Rabbit, and who would be bringing crackers and "pumice" to the party, which Elsie thought sounded pretty gross. She remembered once getting a wart on her foot, and her mommy spent a week or two scratching it off with pumice. Elsie had never thought to taste the pumice, as it was like a light brick. But Mrs. Daryl didn't comment; she simply marked it on her own list and then looked up at Elsie.

"How about you, Elsie? What are you going to bring to the party?"

Elsie hadn't thought of anything; she was too caught up in planning. She felt the eyes of the class on her and looked down at her list as if it could help her. She wiggled her galoshes-free toes in search of epiphany. "Probably something with pumpkin in it!" Someone called out from behind her. Much of the class laughed at this, even Rabbit James.

Elsie blushed. Her ears went cherry red as though they were hot irons. Mrs. Daryl looked around, only partly bemused, then put a hand on Elsie's desk to create a kind of intimacy.

"How about cookies. Do you think your mother has time to make you cookies?"

Elsie didn't so much nod as let her face slowly shudder toward her desk. She stared down at her list of Plan A's as the laughter died down. Mrs. Daryl continued down the line, but Elsie's ears still burned, ringing from the suddenness of the sound. She had been called Pumpkin ever since career day at the beginning of the year, when her daddy had brought in a bunch of pumpkins

and advertisements for Harvest Festivities. Brochures with photos of large piles of pumpkins. The corn maze. T-shirts with the
logo of her daddy's farm. Apple cider that was made locally with
their apples. He didn't really tell them about his career so much
as advertise. He also brought everyone a pumpkin eraser that
attached to the end of their pencil. Everyone snickered at Elsie,
who had to wear an over-large T-shirt advertising the farm. And
of course, Daddy didn't say anything about the trolls.

At recess, Elsie sat on the steps outside the school, all alone,
listening to the distant but empty noise of her schoolmates' fun
playing kickball and finishing up her list. She had scribbled
COOKIES across her page in class because she wanted to remember
to ask her mommy. But the cookies being on the list gave her the
idea that cookies could be her way to meet the trolls.

—

Elsie made it through the rest of the day with minimal interactions,
as she usually did. But she did talk to her friend Lispy Sally at lunch
about Disney princesses. They disagreed about which was the
least pretty. Lispy Sally believed that it had to be "Thnow White,"
because Sally didn't think black hair was pretty, even though she
had black hair too. Elsie thought that it was Cinderella, for running
away once the spell began to fade away.

On the bus ride to her mommy's place, Elsie thought about the
trolls, about her newly revised Plan A for Action, which involved
making cookies with her mommy and going to her daddy's for the
weekend, then sneaking off early Saturday morning, when her
Daddy would probably still be sleeping. She might even leave a
note telling him she went out to play in the maze so he would go

waste time trying to find her there. She imagined the reactions of the trolls and everything else that would happen: how they would accept her, how they would take her to see the golden, magical halls in their "troles," how she would become their princess, how she would become rich, in love—and how she too would learn to hate the pumpkins cluttering up her realm.

——

When Elsie got off the bus, her mommy was waiting, leaning against a brick wall. She came over to give Elsie a big hug. Mommy looked very tired and smelled like vegetables and cold. She worked in a grocery store, in the back, packing and sorting things. Elsie had once gone there with her for Take Your Daughter to Work Day and watched her mommy toil and sweat and get yelled at, while Elsie mostly just sat on a pile of russet spuds. Elsie hadn't liked it there.

Elsie's mommy brushed a hand softly against Elsie's cheek. On the walk to the apartment, Elsie told Mommy about her day at school. She said that it was very fun and she was continuing to make new friends, and she named off a few, like Bickett and Fonz. None of the names were kids in her class. The list she was writing in her mommy's head was endless.

When they got to her mommy's place, they sat on the couch and turned on the television, already tuned to the channel where they always watched shows about reality, with the volume still fairly low. Elsie's mommy sat near her and hugged Elsie while they watched, as she always did, her arms wrapping around and gently scratching, sleepily, at Elsie's belly. Her mommy's apartment building stank of spices and smoke, and there were bugs in the walls, and Elsie could hear people yelling at each other in weird languages. In the winter, the furnaces in the whole building clanged into one long, creepy song. The farm, on the other hand, smelled pretty, and there were no bugs in the walls and there was no smoke. It was the quiet Elsie was raised on, and since her mommy had stopped living there, the quiet was more uninterrupted. Elsie didn't much like her mommy's place, but mommy was there, and Elsie liked being with her best. Watching television with her mommy, Elsie waited for a chance to ask about the cookies and then ask about going to her daddy's place for the weekend, but she didn't want her mommy to think Elsie didn't want to stay with her. She just didn't want to miss the trolls, and she was running out of time. And she'd already had a very loud day.

Did your daddy give you the cheque? her Mommy eventually asked her, after nodding up from a brief nap. Elsie said yes and went to her book bag, which she'd left on the kitchen table. Her mommy slowly rose to follow. Mommy was thin and exhausted all the time from working ten hours a day, five days a week, while trying to sleep in a noisy, lonely place. Elsie handed her mommy the slip of paper that her daddy had itched out.

As her mommy studied the cheque, Elsie asked if they could make some monster cookies together. Elsie said she wanted to have some cookies to share with her friends from school, who, she said, were going to take a hayride through the pumpkin patch that weekend and would maybe even try the corn maze that Elsie, as always, had completely memorized. She said they had been excited to do it since career day. Elsie's mommy looked up at her from the cheque.

So you want to go back for the weekend?

"Only for the Harvest Festivities," Elsie said, hugging her mommy around the waist. Elsie didn't want to tell her mommy about trying to meet the trolls, because she didn't want her mommy to say she couldn't do it. She knew she couldn't break her mommy's spoken rules, so she had to prevent them from being spoken.

Elsie's mommy said that it was fine, and she started to open cabinets, quietly pulling out all the things they needed for the cookies: oatmeal, sugar, vanilla, and all the rest. She moved slowly. She had Elsie help take out some of the things they needed. Once everything was out on the counters, from baking sheets to eggs to measuring cups, Elsie's mommy sat down at the tiny kitchen table and put her head down. Elsie looked over at her, with a wooden mixing spoon in her hand. Her mommy was smiling, but her eyes were almost closed. Elsie asked if she was okay, and Mommy said: *Yes, yes, I'm okay. It's just been so long since we made cookies together. I am happy and tired about it.*

It had been a long time. Elsie had not made cookies with her since Mommy moved out. Her mommy didn't make cookies anymore because she had so little time or energy after working so much during the week. Elsie's daddy, of course, never made Elsie cookies either. Her daddy was as boring a baker as he was a cook. Every meal she had with him tasted the same.

Elsie's mommy kept her head on the table but told Elsie what to do, taught her how to tell the difference between sugar and baking powder by texture: *Sugar is like sand; baking powder like butterfly wings. Flour is like that too, for future reference*, she said. They settled for white chocolate chips because it was all they had. Mommy walked Elsie through preheating the oven and only got up when the whole concoction was ready to show Elsie how to measure out the perfect, monstrous-sized ball for each cookie, how to slip the trays into the hot oven and set the timer.

Elsie's mommy was all smiles and yawns. Elsie knew that her mommy smiled a lot when she was sad. They sat and watched a bit more reality TV, a show about a woman who talked to dead people, while they waited for the cookies to be ready. Her mommy nodded off by the time the alarm chimed, so Elsie, having studied her mommy all her life, went to the oven, donned the oven mitts, and pulled the cookie sheets out and put them on the counter. She closed the oven and even hit the red button to turn it off. She looked at her mommy sleeping on the couch in her powdery apron, and Elsie thought that maybe she herself was the mommy. She went to the phone, took off the right mitten and grabbed the receiver in the left, and dialled the number of her daddy's house. When he answered, Elsie told him she was going to come back sometime that night because she wanted to enjoy the Harvest Festivities that weekend. He said that was fine, but he might be out of the house when she came. He was just on his way to pose the pumpkins on the stairlike levels of the square hay bales that tourists from the city in cardigans and scarves liked to get their pictures taken in front of. He was getting ready for another big weekend.

Elsie put the mittens back on and walked around the tiny apartment as she waited for the cookies to cool. Her mommy snored quietly. Elsie walked over to the bed and stood on it with her oven mitts in the air, and she whispered to herself, "I am the troll princess, I am the mommy of trolls, and I will not turn away when my magic disappears, because I am beautiful." She was happy she didn't have the black hair to contradict it.

When the cookies cooled, Elsie took off her mittens and filled a plastic bag full with the cookies. She put the bag and her backpack by the door and carefully readied her galoshes, as though they were made of magic glass, before going over to wake up her mommy. They should probably get going, Elsie told her. They were both tired, and daddy was expecting her soon.

—

Her mommy drove her. On the drive she told Elsie that she was growing up well, and that she was sorry she'd fallen asleep. But Elsie was used to it. Her mommy had been exhausted forever, though she'd gotten even more so since the divorce. As they drove out of the city, a fog began to drop. Elsie could almost feel the trolls crawling from their troles to finish off the pumpkin patch in the moonlight, and she clutched her cookies—her gift to them. Elsie's mommy stopped the car at the end of the private copse that the driveway passed through and that made the farm invisible from the highway. Her mommy always stopped the car there when she dropped Elsie off, because it was the first place you could get a clear look at the farmhouse. She always waited there until Elsie had made it in the door. She didn't like driving close to the farm, even though it was easier to turn her car around nearer to the house.

When Elsie got out, the fog was too thick for her to see all the way to the door. *Be sure to flip the porch lights on and off once you've made it,* her mommy said, and Elsie said, "I will." *And call me tomorrow, or sometime on Sunday, and tell me about the hayride and all the fun you had with your friends, okay?* And Elsie said, "I will." *Remember, I'm always here for you, so all you have to do is call me. Okay? I will come and get you. Okay? I love you so much, Elsie. Okay?*

Then Elsie climbed back up on the seat and kissed her mommy and then dropped onto the gravel and was off.

The fog was thick, but Elsie followed the crackly driveway. She could only see blurry lights, the porch lights, her mommy's headlights, and the moon. Luckily the walk from the car to the house was pretty straight, and she could tell through her feet whether she was walking on the driveway or had wandered onto the grass. Unlike most people her age, she wasn't afraid of the dark, because the dark was more often a very gentle and quiet thing to her. When she got to the house, her daddy was in the kitchen, cooking something that smelled like every other meal he'd ever made. She said hello to him, clomped her galoshes lightly, and went to the porch light and flicked it on and off three times, leaving it off on the last. She opened the door to watch the headlights sinking back into the trees, leaving behind no light but the blurry moon.

She went inside and put her bag of cookies down on the table. Her daddy said HOWDY and turned back to his food. He seemed frustrated, cursing the meat as he cooked it. He told her, as the pan's hot oil spat up at him, that he was very weary from working that day, so she would be sent to bed soon after supper. Elsie was fine with that, because she had plans to get up early.

In her room, she sat on her bed, painting her fingernails and toenails green with polish she'd bought with her mommy once. She wanted to fit in with the trolls. She made a bit of a mess of it. Before she went to bed, she spent some time looking out her window, in her pyjamas, watching the darkness misting over the corn maze. She fell asleep recalling the routine of twists and turns and misdirects she'd have to take to get to the end. While she slept, she dreamt in silent green.

She got up at predawn as planned and put her hair in a ponytail to be sure it would be fully out of the way. She put on her big sweater and snuck down the stairs, the staticky hairs of her pony-tail drawing themselves to the walls. Her daddy hardly ever got up early, especially not during the harvest, so she felt safe. She had heard him clomping around and talking to the television as she fell asleep the night before, so he had probably gone to bed pretty late, as usual. Her daddy made most of their money from selling the pumpkins and the apples in the self-pick orchard, and from the Harvest Festivities. So as long as he parked the empty trucks in the field the day before, he didn't have to do much for work until the farm opened up around ten for people to come visit. Then, he'd dress up in stained overalls she never saw him wear the rest of the year and would talk to visitors in a slow, fake voice as he walked around with a pitchfork or drove his little tractor with his empty apple cart filled with tools, as though he were a real farmer en route to somewhere. Her daddy hadn't, at least as far as Elsie remembered, ever done much dirty work. And he almost always, at least since the divorce, slept in far beyond the troll's harvest.

In the kitchen, Elsie closed up the bag of monster cookies. Four had been raided by her daddy, despite her having told him that she was saving them for her friends. But there was nothing she could do about that. Her daddy always did what he thought was good, and that was how things went. It was a sacrifice she'd had to accept. Elsie put on her galoshes.

Outside was cool, and Elsie hugged herself in her sweater. The fog was there, and it was a beautiful morning for troll sighting, likely one of the last of the year. The harvest was going quicker this

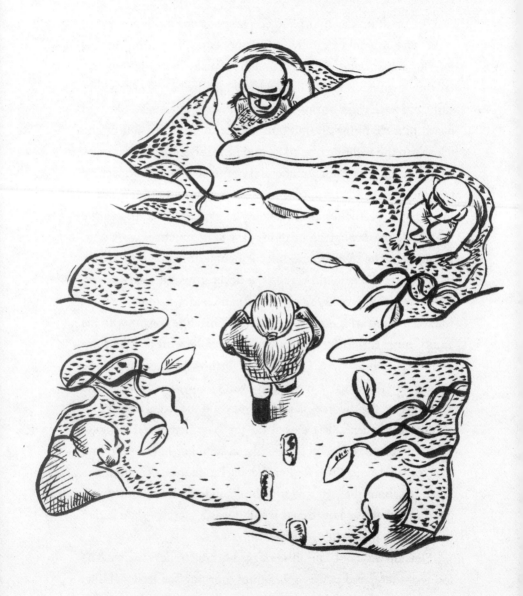

year, and Elsie supposed it had something to do with her daddy buying an extra trailer for the pumpkins.

Finally, Elsie walked into the pumpkin patch for the first time since she was four. The first step was like sneaking into an old, forbidden world. The fog was similarly thick, and the rising sun was nothing but a thin orange streak shining through it. The sun at its absolute brink in the morning and during twilight always reminded Elsie of a giant pumpkin sinking into black earth, so much so that every day and night, she thought of the trolls.

The pumpkins were almost completely picked. Elsie kept walking, the bag of monster cookies clasped in her chilly hands, passing vacant sprawling vine after vacant sprawling vine. She should have worn her winter mittens and her hat, but she was too far gone now to turn back. The cold, wet soil was slapping and attaching itself to her boots. Her feet were getting heavy, but she plodded on, unable to see more than twenty feet ahead of her. She walked straight east, toward the pumpkin-orange streak that peeked from over the trees: her destination.

—

Elsie was already surrounded by the time she noticed the first troll ahead of her. She had been preparing herself not to be afraid, but it hardly helped. She really didn't want the trolls to think she was afraid of them, but they were still so strange to her. When she opened the bag of cookies, they tightened in around her. She was scared, but she didn't want to run, because she knew that would only spook them but even more so because she knew she couldn't run—she was surrounded, and she had all that wet soil attached to her feet. It was easier to convince herself she didn't want to do what she couldn't do anyway.

As the trolls got close—there must have been about twenty—she began to hand out the cookies, hands shaking as each troll accepted a cookie in his mouth, just like that one from when Elsie was four had. None bit into the cookies; they just clasped them in their lips. They looked her over, each as short as she had been at four, each one a green bulge of slouched muscle, each indistinct from his brother. She tried looking around for that first troll she'd met, but as they stood around her, they each seemed to be him and not.

One poked at the wet soil on her galoshes as if it offended him, another seemed to note her heavy breathing, and a third put his curious, gentle hand on her shoulder as if to stop her nervous fidgeting. The trolls surrounded her, with more emerging from the dense fog until she couldn't see the ground at all anymore, the patch being blotted out by the fog and the rippling lake of their backs.

She tried to say hello to them. "Hi, my name is Elsie, who are you? Can you show me where you live? I'd like to see your troles!" But the trolls did not respond. Not even the ones who didn't have a mouthful of cookie. Those few would pantomime opening their wide mouths toward her, mouths that moved to silent syllables and were set between an overhanging brow—concealing pale-yellow eyes—and downward hooking noses and cleft chins. They seemed much more bashful and curious than Elsie remembered. They made no sound except the subtle squish of their feet in the dirt, though somehow they all appeared perfectly clean, as if they had never been soiled by it.

The patch was silent until Elsie's little giggle at being lifted up onto the backs of the trolls. Slowly, they made a procession to the east, toward the widening orange glow. Time was passing, and the fog was lifting. Elsie could finally see that the train of trolls did end, though there were two or three times as many as she had first thought. She definitely hadn't made enough cookies. As they progressed, stragglers at the back of the pack stumbled over pumpkins, picked them up over their heads, and hurried to the nearest truck. There was so little orange visible in the patch between the dry pumpkin leaves and the bodies of trolls that Elsie could hardly believe it had been full of pumpkins no more than a week before, when she'd walked out into the morning fog and seen the first trolls of the season. Now there was nearly nothing left. She jostled and giggled as they silently carried her, heavy boots and all, toward the edge where the patch met the forest.

Her eyes took their time adjusting to the dark. It was then that she realized that the trolls could likely see in the dark. They were nocturnal! That explained so much. Perhaps they were like bats and their speech was supersonic so that nobody else could hear them in the night. Perhaps that was how they hunted prey— providing they ate meat at all. Elsie wasn't sure. They certainly didn't seem to eat cookies.

The sun broke through the trees in sharp, stabbing shafts of brightness. The trolls began to hurry, and Elsie thought that per- haps she had slowed them down. She heard the stragglers sprint- ing up from behind and looked back, her eyes finally able to make out objects out in the darkness of the canopy. She saw the long procession of what must have been fifty little rushing bodies. They made their way down through the trees, and Elsie didn't bother trying to speak to them anymore. She figured that they weren't really the talkative kind, or if they were, maybe only dogs could hear them.

They piled down the side of a river valley. Elsie knew this river because it cut around to the edge of their property, near the exit of the corn maze. The river wasn't safe for swimming—that was what Elsie's daddy told her. He said there were bad things in it that you should never touch. Once she had seen dead fish after dead fish floating by, fish who must have mistakenly spawned up the river to mate. Her daddy said that the river carried some sort of hex, and that was probably where the trolls came from. Her mommy, when Elsie told her about the river, said this hex was pesticides.

As they walked along the river valley, Elsie began to catch a whiff of a great stink. On the top of the valley, she noticed a pile of garbage bags and trolls searching through them, some slowly coming down the slope to join the march home. One had a makeshift clay bowl filled with stinky cubed meat, and another had a bag of rotting broccoli that seemed to have been bought but never opened. Soon, as the sun began to spill toward them, the clan came upon holes in the earth in the side of the river valley, each surrounded by rocks to visually accentuate their presence. Little green faces popped in and out of them. These were their troles! Elsie's throng came upon them, some twenty openings, and divided their entrance between them. Elsie was set down on the ground in front of one, where her galoshes were cleaned by a few trolls with wet, frayed rags before a small group of trolls ushered her to follow them inside.

Inside the trole was darkness again, but they left a single doorway open so that Elsie would eventually be able to see, though even that much light seemed to make the rest of the trolls have to squint their beautiful yellow eyes. Within the trole was a great, dank hall, and there were troll women and troll children there too. The troll women were much the same as the troll men, only thinner, with longer hair, little muscle, and sagged breasts. The children were the size of human babies and stood a bit more upright than their elders. The faces of the women and children were, if anything, more cavernous and bony than the men's. Elsie realized that *all* of the trolls, not only the women and children, appeared to be so strong because there was nothing on their bodies *but* muscle. She realized that their backs were not bent from carrying weight, but from hunger.

Each of the trolls Elsie had given a cookie to went up to the long table surrounded by sitting stones and took the monster cookie out of his mouth and placed it there. Women and children gathered, and it was then that Elsie noticed, at the back of the hall, where the light barely licked, her mommy's cookie jar, which the trolls had taken several years ago, was sitting on a kind of altar.

The trolls' attention was directed toward Elsie; they made mouth movements to their neighbours and pointed. They did not look Elsie in the eye though, or approach her once she was in that wide, short hall. But they seemed to be communicating about her, and one of the male trolls, as indistinct to Elsie as the rest, stood up on the short table and moved his mouth as if he were speaking. The rest listened to his impassioned, silent speech, watching as he gestured toward the altar that held the cookie jar and to the feast

on the table, where the trolls had also placed the rotting broccoli
and the festering meat.

And then, almost in a blink, the trolls began to dance, and
they began to sing—or, at least, they appeared to sing. Elsie felt
like Snow White, and these little green people were her unnamed
dwarfs. They did not move much when they danced, but they all
seemed to be moving in the rhythm of a sound that she could not
hear. She only heard their feet softly falling as they moved back and
forth, sometimes taking an opportunity of great energy to stand
at full height and cease to bend their backs. They were moving
in circles around Elsie, and she looked on from green face to
green face, from altar to table. As she stood in the centre of their
dancing, Elsie suddenly was able to tell the differences between
each of them, to tell them apart from one another, and as she did,
she realized something about the trolls that she had not been able
to notice before: they were dying. But they were dancing for her,
nonetheless. She wished more than anything to be able to hear
them. She focused her ears, tried to tune in to their song so that she
might join in the dance in her shimmering galoshes. She listened,
and, finally, a screaming outside voice was heard, cutting through:
HEY, YOU LITTLE GREEN RATFUCKS, WHERE THE HELL DID
YOU PUT MY DAUGHTER?

Elsie heard her father's voice bounce down against the bank of
the valley and into the open mouth of the trole. She had forgotten
to leave the note saying she was in the maze. The trolls froze in
their dance as soon as a shadow overtook the mouth of the cave,
a big shadow—with a large gun—cut off above the knees because
her father had to stand down the slope to see inside. The silhouette of his bearded face was animated and seemed to be gesturing

for Elsie to come forward into the light. She couldn't hear him anymore—at first she thought it was because the sound of her heart pumping in her ears was drowning him out, but then she realized it was because her father's voice could no longer reach her. It was like her Mommy had explained: *At some point me and your daddy just couldn't talk to each other anymore.*

Elsie and her father were finally at separate registers. She couldn't move; she was terrified, terrified of the silence that had swallowed her daddy's screaming, unsure even if she could still hear her own voice but deciding, with faith, that she could. Dimly, as her father began to point the gun and as the trolls slunk away from her, she heard a grumbling emerge from the quiet. As her father readied his eye to the gun, Elsie was goaded forward by a gentle finger to her rib.

Softly, a green voice: Go, child.

MIDAS'S HAIRDRESSER

IN AN OLD PIECE OF LUGGAGE BENEATH HER BED, Midas's hairdresser kept every piece of gold that Midas had paid her with over the last six months. Each piece was oddly shaped and incongruously sized. Some of their edges were rounded, while others were sharp. She hid the gold under the bed because she was hoping to discover what they might amount to, aside from millions and millions of dollars. Eventually, she thought, the pieces might make up some whole—some quotidian artifact that Midas had accidentally mishandled during the three weeks that followed Dionysus granting him the golden touch. Midas had been granted one wish for agreeing not to press charges after Dionysus's satyr friend Silenus broke into Midas's penthouse on a dare. Midas had wished that everything he touched would turn to gold. Three weeks later, after Midas found he could no longer live with the power he'd dreamt of—the power to make money all his own—Dionysus cleansed him of the golden touch. Now a self-made billionaire, Midas then cut up some mysterious gold-touched thing into pieces small enough that he could use them to pay for everyday things like shoeshines, ribeyes, taxi rides, or her backroom cut 'n' shaves.

Midas had insinuated something that hinted at such a summation to his butcher, and his butcher had told his taxi driver, who then told her. All Midas's tradespeople talked with each other. Midas had said to the butcher, while handing over a small, obtuse nugget in exchange for a fine rack of lamb, "Just you wait until you see what I butchered to get this!"

The hairdresser wasn't sure she really believed that the pieces would add up to anything, but curiosity made her keep it up. Made her keep quiet about it.

———

Midas's hairdresser knew Midas's secret: that Apollo had cursed him to grow the ears of an ass—of course—but more importantly, that he had taken a secret lover. For the last few months, she'd seen Midas sneaking around in his large, floppy Gucci hat—which was clearly hiding something—and calling upon a young blond man who lived at the end of her street. She knew the young man was a hustler, and she knew that Midas wouldn't take a taxi all the way down to the village just to have coffee and a chat.

None of this was surprising to her. When you go through a phase in your life where you can indiscriminately turn refuse into gold, you reach an inconceivable level of fame. Of brashness to act however you please. As soon as you grow out of a trait like that, people flock to sell themselves to you, hoping they might suck some of the foam off the top of your wealth—being wary only of shaking your hand in case you learn how to transmute people into gold again. Even the most appalling and foolish person—James E. Midas—could garner that kind of interest.

Midas's hairdresser knew that it would be bad for business if she told anyone about Midas's ass ears or his lover. Especially not Midas's wife, who allegedly hadn't let Midas touch her since he'd accidentally turned his seventeen-year-old daughter—her step-daughter—into $40 million worth of lifeless metal. He'd forgotten himself and tapped his daughter on the shoulder to ask if she wanted to borrow his BMW, which was said to have a solid-gold steering wheel, radio knob, key, gear shift, and driver's side door. Midas himself told his hairdresser the whole story one afternoon, when—in the backroom of her salon, locked—she was once again perfecting his hair and buzzing the short fur of his ass ears into a gentle, felty fuzz.

"She doesn't get it," Midas said to his hairdresser, as he turned his head side to side, stroking and picking at his ears, checking himself in the mirror before paying her—as usual—with a small, odd-shaped shard of gold. The story he told was much different than the one she'd already heard in the tabloids.

—

When she smoked on the fire escape at night, where she couldn't hear the TV, or her wife yelling at the fear-mongering political candidates, or the fear-mongering news about the fear-mongering candidates, she could see Midas—dressed plain, besides that ridiculous hat—slipping down her street and into his lover's home. Most nights he didn't go there, but whenever he did, she caught him, always around 11:15, plus or minus one or two cigarettes.

She would watch him amble down the street in that floppy hat, his pockets weighed down. She'd often chuckle at the way his pants were drooping from all the gold he carried. He wore two pairs of suspenders. He looked insane. And once he reached the end of the street, he'd knock, and the door would open, and the young blond man—who had visited her shop once, despite it being on Madison Avenue, and who had paid her with a small gold cube for a routine bangs trim—would rush him across the jamb.

The hairdresser didn't tell anyone about the lover, or the ass ears, because she knew that would only lead to the media learning about it, which would only lead to Midas getting a divorce. A divorce would mean his wife taking much of his gold, which would leave Midas's hairdresser in the lurch. Each of Midas's tradespeople was afraid of how his wife could ruin them, should she ever decide to leave him.

Midas's hairdresser used the excuse that she was saving up for her and her wife's retirement, even though that had been set soon after Midas began hiring her. The real reason she was worried about keeping him as her client was that she was waiting for the pieces of gold to take some sort of shape. Midas and his wife had already nearly split up when he tragically turned his daughter into gold two weeks into having his golden touch, and they'd inched even closer a few months later, after Midas, having been made a judge on *American Idol* following the story of his meteoric rise in wealth going viral, said that between the final two contestants, Apollo and Pan, Apollo's voice was not as good as Pan's because Apollo's was perfect and therefore less interesting than Pan's wavering croon.

"That's what made Apollo curse me to wake up one morning with the ears of an ass," Midas confessed to his hairdresser the first time she trimmed his hairy ears in the backroom, which was why he'd begun wearing the silly Gucci hat all the time. His wife tolerated the hat because it was finely made, by a good name, but she valued perfection too much to ever tolerate the news of the ears reaching the public. The real problem his wife had with him wasn't the ass ears, but that she had loved Apollo's voice and wanted him to win.

—

But ever since Midas began trusting his hairdresser with his ears and paying her in gold, the hairdresser had been having bad dreams. In her wife's arms, she imagined herself running down the streets and screaming about the ears, about Midas's infidelity, and she pictured Midas looming over her, dripping golden tears upon her—which she caught greedily. His hairdresser was haunted by the knowledge of both his secrets because she knew she couldn't tell anyone. Meanwhile, being the only one who knew those secrets caused her to question the truth of them herself. She felt crazy. When she did people's hair, including Midas's wife's, she diverted conversation away from Midas—a popular topic in the city—to discuss the Kardashians or, god help her, politics. *Can you believe what that prick said about immigration?*

Midas's hairdresser bit her tongue, though she wanted to scream everything she knew about Midas. She was tightly pressurized with what she knew. She couldn't even tell her own wife what she knew, that she dealt with him, that they were millionaires, that it was only a matter of time until the pieces all added up to something and she could, with the satisfaction of knowing yet another secret, sell off the gold for an estate in the country, perhaps out in the Hamptons, and *freedom*. What politics could get to them then, with all that money? By then she must have had nearly two hundred pounds of gold, because to Midas at one point, money *had* grown on trees—so long as he made sure to touch them.

—

One night around 11:20, Midas's hairdresser, restlessly chain-smoking while her wife was screaming and breaking plates and throwing books in the apartment to the tempo of a rerun of the presidential debate, saw Midas slipping to his lover's once again—like clockwork—but at that moment something clicked, and she decided she had to do something about this overwhelming knowledge, this overflowing secret she'd been asked to bear for so long, when her instinct was *always* to tell. So she went back into the apartment and watched her wife for a moment—she was breaking a dining room chair in half, sobbing—before going out the door and down onto the street. She went to the park a few blocks away and, in an empty clearing, dug a small, shallow hole with her hands. Into this hole she whispered the secrets: "Midas has the ears of an ass and a beautiful blond lover." After replacing the dirt, she felt an almost orgasmic relief, as if she had just hurled sickness into the earth and become instantly cured of it.

Every night for a week, she came down to the park, to this same spot of earth, dug, and reiterated the secret, adding detail upon detail, until she'd said it all. She felt a lightness. She buzzed Midas's ear hair again and got yet another piece of gold, which she took back to her messy apartment, still trashed from her wife's fury. She pulled the piece of luggage out from under the bed. She set all the pieces on the floor and tried again to put them together, and finally, it began to make sense. It seemed that what she had was a large, round golden foot. But she still wasn't sure who it might belong to. Her curiosity was still hungry, so she put the gold back under the bed and kept wondering what it could all mean.

On the following Tuesday, the fear-mongering news that she kept playing in her salon was focused differently. It told this time of the tragic death of the woman who had been married to Midas.

The night before, Midas's wife had been trampled to death in their penthouse by what seemed to be—in Midas's security footage—a large golden hippopotamus. The tracks of the beast led back to a small patch of earth in a park seven blocks away, continued through the house, and disappeared into the river. Midas had reportedly said to press that he'd been spared only because he'd been out buying seltzer water from the 7-Eleven down the street when it happened. No one believed him, and word began to spread about his likely infidelity. The hairdresser watched as a live helicopter shot showed the huge impressions made in the cement and the asphalt by a hugely dense, solid-gold pachyderm. At the same moment, she heard the helicopter flying above the streets outside her salon.

When she got home that night, Midas's hairdresser found marks on the hardwood floor from where the pieces of gold had dragged themselves out of the luggage under the bed, through the hall, and gnawed their way through the bottom of the door to get out to the street. She blamed not noticing it that morning on the general disarray of their apartment and her increasing desire to escape as quickly as possible every morning.

The first thing she did was to call the butcher, who was weeping: "All gone, all gone." Midas's hairdresser chain-smoked in terror. Midas did not come out that night to see his lover, whose building had also been ransacked by the hippopotamus that afternoon. It was still on the loose. Breaking news stories claimed that if the hippopotamus was in fact solid gold, it would weigh around two hundred thousand pounds and be worth billions of dollars. "We should elect the hippo to the presidency!" the anchor's muffled voice said, as Midas's hairdresser stood out on the fire escape and smoked. Her wife came back from work late, noticed the holes in the door and the grooves running down the stairs, and asked why the place was in a more terrible state than when she had left it.

"The worst of them got the candidacy," the hairdresser told her wife, who without responding went into the other room to hopelessly scream and destroy their home in solitude. Meanwhile, on the street, a large golden form appeared from out of the dark. It was pointing its multibillion-dollar snout up at the increasingly unwealthy woman on the fire escape, and Midas—his hat nowhere to be seen—was perched on its back, weeping big golden tears, his ass ears flopping.

Once the hairdresser's wife wore herself out destroying their home, the solid-gold hippo finished it off by tearing out the foundation. Cathartically, it fell down on top of them all.

PATHETIC FALLACY

WHILE THEY WROTE about the never-ending snowstorm in the first pages of their novel, outside of their apartment, snow began to fall.

—

It was four days into the snow, into writing their novel, when they realized that it had not stopped snowing since they'd started. Their partner was slipping on her boots and jacket and beanie and gloves to go to the bookstore where she worked. "What're you up to today?" she asked, and they said, looking out at the falling white, "The novel."

—

In the novel, the main character lived in St. Louis and missed true winter, having grown up in northern Minnesota. In the first scene, the main character stood at their window in their apartment overlooking Forest Park and was struck by the memories of having to wear a parka under their Halloween costumes as a child. Memories of door jambs freezing. Memories of walking exactly in the knee-deep pockets of their father's footsteps in the snow as they went out to fell a Christmas tree. It was mid-October when the novel began, when the character was shaken by the sharpest pangs of nostalgia. All the while, outside their window, a blue fall sky began to snow.

It was mid-October when they started writing the novel too. Their apartment building was a similar building, only none of the high Forest Park–facing apartments had been available when they moved in. Their apartment was on the third floor, facing the opposite way.

By the fourth day, the temperature outside had finally gotten cold enough for the snow to stick. There were several inches on the ground. They walked out of the apartment building to see it. On the streets, people shovelled paths in the sidewalk. It felt a little like home to them. After a short walk, watching their breath billow and feeling their lips chap, they went back to the apartment and continued to write.

On day ten there were three feet of snow.

On day thirteen—Halloween—there were seven. Outside the window, they and their partner watched kids dressed as ghosts move like snowdrifts down the snow-blown paths. They watched a miniature Captain America pull a beanie down over his mask. They watched a father carry a tiny Princess Peach wrapped in a blanket, while her mother followed with a tiny jack-o'-lantern bucket.

In the novel, the character saw these same things.

That weekend, their partner was supposed to work, but the bookstore closed. Business slowed to nothing in the non-essential stores in the city. They sat on the couch under a blanket together, drinking tea and watching a marathon of *The Simpsons'* Treehouse of Horror episodes. Their partner snuggled as they took out their phone and sent themselves an email. "Is that for the novel?" she asked, and they said, "Yes."

The novel was about the dangers of nostalgia. The dangers of wanting the world to be a certain remembered way while not understanding what that would entail. The email was a note telling them to introduce other characters into their St. Louis: characters who didn't see snow, but found themselves back in high school or being treated as though they were nine years old again, before their parents' divorce.

While they wrote these stories into the novel, the snow let up a little. Until they returned to the main story, where the snow was never-ending.

—

On day nineteen, half of the city had left, and it was the third day of the state of emergency. The snow was twenty-six feet deep. The news showed flyover footage of St. Louis under a blanket of whiteness that ended at the Mississippi and didn't go farther west than St. Charles. There was snowy footage of houses that had collapsed under the weight of the snow, of abandoned downtown office buildings half-crumpled under the immense weight.

—

"This is all proof that global warming is a hoax," someone said on the news. The next segment was an interview with a family who had lost their home in University City, the camera zooming in on every tear.

—

They spent so much time writing the novel. There wasn't anything else to do. Most of the residents of their building had left, but there were enough still remaining that relief teams dropped food and water and other necessities onto the roof for them. Those left weren't ready to be evacuated. Between writing the novel, they would go out on the roof for a shift of shovelling snow to keep it from accumulating and crushing the building. It was so cold by then that nobody could stay out for more than fifteen minutes at a time.

—

They didn't leave, though. They did not have a car or anywhere to go.

Around day fifteen, their partner started to walk around the frigid apartment in an old cross-country running uniform and thermals. She ran through the halls, up and down the stairs. She'd hardly run since placing second at State in her senior year of high school. While she did, they went up to the twelfth floor and walked into one of the abandoned apartments that overlooked the park. There wasn't really any park to see. The trees had almost all fallen from the weight of the snow. They just sat there and wrote.

"The snow is covering the park. There are twigs staring out from it. The pipes in the building have been bursting for the last three days. It's beautiful and perfect."

On day thirty-three, when they couldn't see out the window of their apartment anymore, they moved into the apartment on the twelfth floor overlooking the park—which had become a bare white plain. It was only two floors down from the roof, and since more people had started to leave—flagging down the relief helicopters as they came to drop off supplies and surrendering themselves to evacuation—they needed to take extra shifts shovelling to keep the roof clear.

Down the hall from their new apartment, there was a family. Parents and a child, from the sounds of them. There was always noise: sometimes childlike laughter, sometimes the parents screaming at one another, sometimes a child sobbing. Whenever either of them walked past the door on their way to the stairway, they swore they could smell something dead inside.

—

Their partner ran and ran. The two of them didn't really talk that much. They woke up together; she dressed in her gear and they bundled up by the window and wrote. Sometimes they woke up together in the middle of the night because of the sounds bouncing down the hall.

—

On day thirty-four, the snow stopped at fifty-seven feet, and they were hit with writer's block. They went to the roof and looked out over the remains of the city, feeling deeply hopeless. They did not write on day thirty-five either, and the temperature started to rise, threatening thaw. They could hardly sleep.

—

On day thirty-eight, their partner asked, "What's wrong?" as she pulled on her running shoes. They said, "I can't write. I'm stuck," and she said, "Do you want me to read it and tell you what I think?"

—

On day forty, the temperature was expected to rise above freezing for the first time in more than a month. Their partner had read the unfinished draft but hadn't told them what she thought. That morning, she put on her cross-country running shoes and said, "You should clear the last of the roof in case the snow starts up again. I'm going on a run."

—

As they cleared the last of the snow, they looked down and saw someone crawl out a window of the building. She was in a cross-country uniform and thermals. They watched as she started to run away from the building at a strong and steady pace. From their perspective, it looked like she slowed down as she got farther away, but they knew that was just a trick of distance. She shrank into the seemingly endless whiteness until it was clear she wasn't going to turn back. Their breath started fogging as the temperature began to drop. The snow started to fall again. The words came back into their head, and they dropped the shovel by the door and went down into the empty apartment to write.

—

"This is unprecedented," the news said about something other than St. Louis. On another channel, a death toll was roughly estimated, and photos of tent cities on the east bank of the Mississippi were shown against the backdrop of a white snow cliff.

—

On the roof, they'd realized that the novel was all wrong. The premise was flawed. They examined the strains of the book: the character who was nostalgic for true winter and found themselves in a city where the snow never ceased; the character who wanted to regain her high school glory and found herself eternally agitated and insecure and stressed out; the elderly character who wanted to return to the age of nine, when his parents were still together, and found himself restless and doted upon by his parents' reanimated corpses between bouts of their foreshadowing fights. As they had watched their partner running over the horizon of their world, they realized that the idea that these characters could each live in their own version of St. Louis at once was wrong. Instead, the best way was not to make their worlds parallel, but perpendicular, because no one's world is free from the interference of another's.

—

On New Year's Eve, day seventy-four, the snow was flush to the roof and rising. There was nowhere to put the snow to keep it from accumulating atop the building. The new draft of the book was finished, and they printed it out with the last of their printer ink and put it in a binder. They packed a bag with the book and the remains of their food and went up to the roof. The snow was a foot deep.

—

Outside, they tied their scarf tighter and began to walk into the blank white. They left deep footprints behind that were quickly covered by the shifting snow. As they walked, they didn't remember following their father through the snow. There were no footprints at all to follow in.

WHICH HOUSE?

"I DIDN'T WANT TO HAVE SEX EVERY TIME THAT WE DID," she said to him, as they were finally breaking up for the last time. Their breaking up and getting back together felt to him like pulling green branches from a tree with his bare hands. It felt like doing violence to something that was alive. It felt like doing violence to something young that would likely live on after, or come back wounded.

But that sentence was the axe. It cut quick and clean. After she said it, after he paused and processed, he apologized to her. He hadn't known that—everything had just been so quietly fucked up for so long. He'd not known, but he didn't ask her to elaborate. She said it was okay. It was the end and it was okay. Then, he said, "I guess I'll go," and left her apartment.

Her sentence followed him. It followed him down the stairs to the curb outside her building, where he stood looking across the street at a stumpy little one-storey house that he'd never noticed before, a little house that was crammed between a bright two-storey with a wraparound porch and a six-unit railroad-style apartment building like the one he'd just left for the last time. The house looked like it was about to fall apart. The roof was caving in. The door looked a little off its hinges. It had that soaked-wood kind of colour as it sat there in the shadows on its scraggly lawn, surrounded in a spare copse of maple trees. Did someone live there? Had he ever seen them? He wanted to turn around and call up to her with the intercom, not to ask for more information but to simply tell her again that he was sorry, that he'd not known, not really, and that he was mortified to his core. But he knew that if he called her up on the intercom, he would just end up asking her about that house. He was afraid of what she would say. He was afraid that she would ask him "Which house?" and he would turn around from the intercom and find the house gone.

No, he didn't do it. He stopped looking at the house and then walked down the street and caught the city bus home. Within the week he was on the plane, leaving Canada for Bangkok. For the whole flight, her seat was empty beside him.

—

In Bangkok, he taught English to Thai kids who were proficient in a language he'd likely never learn. After teaching, he went back to the little apartment he'd rented because there was enough space for two. He filled the space with cases of Singha beer and drank it looking out the window at the city, trying to feel grief over what he'd lost, but instead he felt like he'd been gnawed hollow. Depression moved in and took up her side of the bed.

After a year teaching there, he met another expat, whom he let smile and flirt with him. He was slow with her. He let her kiss him. He let her hold his hand as they walked through the crowded markets. He let her meet him outside of the school after work and drink from a bottle in his apartment. But as soon as she started to try and touch him, he got scared. He said he wasn't ready for that yet and he didn't tell her why.

For one class, he had the idea of taking his students on a walk through the neighbourhood and pointing out things and giving the English words for them. To tack his foreign language into their known world. "Lamppost," he said. "Sidewalk," he gestured. "Motorcycle." "Woman." After he told them the words, he quizzed them. "Sidewalk." "Car." "Dog." And then, just as they were finishing their circuit, across from the school—between a restaurant and a two-storey complex peppered with AC units—the squat, falling-apart house was there. It stood out especially because it did not have a gated fence, as so many of the buildings did in the city. Instead of the little maples, there was a small copse of palm trees. He stopped, and the class stopped behind him. They all looked at the house. He looked at his class. They were all smiling and innocent. He pointed at the house.

"House," one kid said.

"Which house," another kid said, followed by others joining her chorus. "Which house!" "Which house!" "Which house!"

"No," he said, quieting them down. "We do not use 'which' here. It is just 'house.' Or maybe 'that house.'"

After school, the expat girl came to meet him and held up a plastic bag and smiled. Beer. Children yelled and laughed and screamed in a flow around him, brushing past him. He looked beyond her at the house, which he had never noticed there before, the house that looked so much like the one he'd seen across the street from his ex's apartment but that he told himself could not be the same house.

He thought of pointing it out to her, but he didn't.

"Shall we?" she said. "My place?"

"Sure," he said, as she strung her arm in his. When they got to her place, she opened the beers and they drank. They made dinner together. She kissed him. She kissed his neck. She pulled up his shirt. He asked her, "Do you really want to do this?" And she looked up at him and unbuckled his belt and said, "What do you think?" He didn't answer. He thought about a disintegrating veranda.

After, she went into the bathroom, and he went to the fridge and pulled out two more beers. He opened them and went to the window by the bed and held them, looking out at the darkening street, seeing Bangkok's downtown skewer the sky behind. He drank from one of the beers and then noticed, on the rooftop of a building across the street: the house. He stared at it, feeling every hair on his body standing on end, as if each follicle were trying to pull itself from the burning ship of his body. As he stood there, staring at the house, she came back from the bathroom and wrapped herself around him. Kissed his back.

"Do you see that house? On that roof?"

"Which house?" She asked, squinting, then going over to get her glasses. But as she was walking back, the house rose on two lizard-like legs. It stood there, pointing toward him with its door closed, and as she put on her glasses and came back to him at the window, the house turned around and leapt off the building.

She stood beside him, squinting behind the glasses.

"Which house?"

The next day, he called her, as he stood outside of his place, staring at the house again, this time set between the two across the street. On the other side of the world, he'd seen those same degrading boards as he left his ex's apartment building. He could still be that man. "I don't think we should see each other anymore," he said, and she started to cry "I'm sorry," he said, and she hung up on him. He put the phone down, still staring at the house. An older Thai woman he recognized as living in the neighbourhood was walking by with a small dog and a plastic sack in her hand. When she made eye contact, he smiled, then pointed at the house.

"Do you know what this house is?"

She stopped beside him and looked across the street to the house, turned back to him, and said, simply and very slowly in English: "Which. House."

By the time he thanked her and looked back across the street, the house was gone, and the buildings beside had filled the place where it had been.

———

Just before his contract to teach English in Thailand ended, a contract he decided not to renew, he sent his ex in Canada an email that said he hoped she was doing well, and ended it with another apology. When she replied, she said she was doing well. She had a new boyfriend. She told him an anecdote about how they met. The anecdote made the boyfriend seem good to her, good for her, good in the right ways. Far, far better than the bad men she'd been with before him, men who had been emotionally abusive to her, men who had told her that she could not do all the things he believed that she could do. The chain of bad men that, now that they had broken up for good—with that sentence—he felt like the last link to. That he hoped he was. At the end of the email telling him about her new boyfriend, she wrote "It's all water under the bridge."

He sat there, his apartment half-packed for his move, with a reply ready to send but which he was not sending: "Did you ever see an old house across the street from your apartment? In a little copse of trees, looking like it was falling apart?"

But he didn't send that. What he ended up sending was: "I am glad your life is going so well. I'm still sorry. I still feel bad."

He did not ask her to elaborate.

———

When he moved back to Canada, he lived on his friend's couch for a few weeks. He thought about going by her apartment to see if the house was there, but he was afraid that she might still live there and might see him. That even though the air between them seemed clear, seeing him might trigger something haunting in her. His friend asked if he'd found a job, and he said he hadn't, not yet. His friend said, "I know a guy who works with a mining exploration company, and they're always looking for people who aren't dolts to work up north."

Within a week, he was on a plane to Rankin Inlet with a group of men who were also heading up to the camp, mostly his age or a few years younger than him. They talked about girls on the plane, about their girlfriends and the extra girls they kept on the side.

Talked about what their go-to drink to send to a girl was. When they asked him, he said that he was single. Not seeing anyone.

They asked him which apps he was on. When he said none, they got excited and began to argue best practices. Many suggested swiping right on every single girl on Tinder and unmatching with anyone he didn't like after matching. They gave him tips for what to do if he wanted to just get fucked. If he wanted to find a girlfriend, they gave him the names of the apps best for that, and tips on how to let any girl looking to hook up know that she could ignore him while not scaring off the rest.

The night they spent in Rankin Inlet, before they were set to take a bush plane to a tiny airstrip in the middle of nowhere three hundred miles north, he thought about the expat in Bangkok and downloaded the apps. He felt shame and dread, like the thought of pollution, but still he made some profiles, following their suggestions to avoid luring hookups, in case he'd want to use them during the two weeks he'd have in civilization after his first four in the field.

The next day, they flew up to the camp in mainland Nunavut, and the next morning, his drill team was dropped off by helicopter to take samples in the tundra twenty miles north of camp. It was summer, but they all wore coats and bug masks because the mosquitoes up there were so intense. While they worked, they saw, through their individual veils of mosquito nets, caribou running in the distance with thick clouds chasing them, stopping every now and again to take a nibble of foliage before moving again. The land was flat, the work straightforward, and the days lasted forever.

Two days later, as he tried to sleep while scratching the bites where the mosquitoes had snuck through his gear, he opened Tinder on his phone. There was no service, no internet, but a face still showed up on the screen. He looked at the picture a long time, a woman named Barbara whose age said twenty-seven and was apparently 1,750 miles away. She had long grey hair and piercing green eyes. She wasn't smiling. She didn't have a bio or any other pictures. He swiped right anyway, and even though he had no internet, they matched.

Barbara: "Hey there."

He put his phone down and didn't reply. Then, he picked up his phone and shut it down.

———

He didn't check the phone again for weeks, until he was heading south on his first break. He didn't tell any of the guys about Barbara, didn't ask if they'd matched with her too. He also didn't tell them about how he'd started to see mirages in the distance when they were drilling, mirages in the form of a tiny copse of tall pine trees peeking over the tundra's horizon. They were at least 150 miles north of the treeline.

He turned on his phone as he sat by the window of the plane to Rankin Inlet. The other guys who were heading back home were sharing the complicated itineraries of drinking and fucking they'd devised to make the most of the next few weeks in the south. He wanted to put on some music to drown them out. He felt sick and included. Felt that they were his kind. That perhaps they too had that same sentence in their pasts. That perhaps they did and it did not worry them.

After he turned the phone on, he turned it to airplane mode right away, but still the notifications came.

Barbara: "Let's not do this."

Barbara: "Come on."

Barbara: "I know you're seeing this ;)"

He didn't reply. He put on his music, then looked at her profile. Her eyes skewered him, and he looked at how far away she was. 1,503 miles. 1,228 miles. 924 miles. 531 miles. 157. 32. <5.

Barbara: "Don't look down!"

They were coming down below the cloud ceiling, beginning their descent toward Rankin, and on the ground near the shadow of the plane was the house, sprinting along. Trailing behind it, the trees—maple and palm and pine and many other trees he'd never seen with the house before—were running on thick root legs. As he looked down, the house turned its door up to look at the plane, and standing in the open doorway in a silver sundress, waving: Barbara.

After he pulled away from the window, a notification pinged his phone.

Barbara: "It's about time you stop ghosting me!"

As he read the notification, the music in his headphones faded out for a moment, just long enough for a voice to say, "See you soon."

―

He walked away from the group in the bright-blue building of the little airport in Rankin Inlet, with its signs in English and Inuktitut, having told the guys he'd be back before their flight south in three hours, that he wanted to say hi to someone. Things started to come together. He walked into town, in no particular direction, knowing that every street would eventually take him to the same place.

The copse around the house had painted trees made of plywood, which was somehow less conspicuous than real trees would have been. The house was the same as it had always been, only now, as he walked across its ratty lawn, it wasn't hiding its legs. They stood at either side, lizard-like but with its claws painted in a bright glitter polish. He didn't knock. There was a light on inside. Barbara had her back to him, wearing the silver sundress. He shut the door behind him.

As soon as he took a step toward Barbara, he felt the house lift itself. As it started to walk, he lost his balance and fell to his knees on the creaky floor. He was surprised he didn't break through the clearly rotting wood. The world blurred by outside the windows.

"บ้านแม่มด," Barbara said, and as she spoke the words in Thai, he remembered what everyone had said about the house, remembered the chorus of Thai kids chanting, "Which house." With what little of the language he knew, he understood then that what she was saying was not "which house."

"Witch house," he said.

"*My* house," Barbara said, turning around. She was no longer her young self and no longer wearing the dress. Her skin was dirty, spotted, weighed down by time. Her breasts long and full and many.

"Who are you? What do you want with me?" he asked.

"That's not how this works," she said. "Or, that's not how it works *this time*. I am many different things for many different people. A symbol of fertility, or Morgan le Fay, or a symbol of death, or Baba Yaga—even Barbara Yaga, if I'm using Tinder."

She winked at him with her deep, humourful, now-milky left eye.

"I am very old and very otherwise," she said, as she walked over and stood by the window, watching the world smear into colour. The house was moving so fast.

"You've hurt people," she said. "And you won't stop, at the rate you're going."

As she looked over at him, on his knees, he put his head down against the floor, and the numbness burst and he began to weep in deep, heaving sobs.

———

The blurry windows began to play his relationship with his ex. Its start while she was still living with a man who'd tried—albeit less than the man before him—to squash her. Old Otherwise paused the replaying now and again to explain some of the complexities, that he had been the other guy, that it had been his first relationship and it couldn't be called a relationship for so long because it was illicit—that it couldn't be called that until after she'd broken up with her boyfriend and then with him too. For the first time. That it couldn't be called a relationship until they got back together. But even then it wasn't. That sex for her was not something meaningful or interesting like it was to him. That he'd known this.

"You were never taught anything," Old Otherwise said. "You were a late bloomer, inexperienced. Your parents never gave you the talk. Your school only taught you abstinence education. You didn't think you would ever find someone else willing to love you because it had taken you this long, so you were desperate to try and keep her even though she was a bad match. Even though she could never be with you as fully as you wanted her to be."

Old Otherwise sat on the floor beside him. She played through their sex scenes, the majority of which he'd completely forgotten, making sure to stop and point out the ones where his ex did not seem all that into it.

"She put up with it, though," Old Otherwise said. "She didn't get much from sex, but she did love you."

But then she played a scene from just after they'd broken up for the first time. He was sick with sadness and frustration and told her that he wanted to see her, and she agreed to come see him but told him before coming over that she didn't want to have sex with him. But by the end, they ended up having sex.

"I can't actually read her mind," Old Otherwise said. "But this is the most damnable episode of the bunch. You thought you'd convinced her to change her mind, but you never really asked her if she had. But she still took you back a few months later."

———

He kept dry heaving until the end, when his ex told him that she hadn't wanted to have sex every time that they did. Old Otherwise put her hand on his back.

"And this is just the *beginning*."

Then, she fast-forwarded his life to the expat in Thailand. She paused and replayed scenes with the expat over and over again.

"She looks very happy, doesn't she? And she was so uncomplicated. And you broke her fucking heart. After sleeping with her for the first time. And you didn't tell her why."

He had his head in his hands. The world blurred out again.

"What can I do? How can I stop it?"

"You can stop it by stopping. The thing that makes you different is that at least you learned your lesson. The lesson has haunted you. You haven't done anything like that since. But because you have always been afraid to sit and look at what you did, the actual reality of what you did, you've hurt other people. In different ways. Innocent people, women, the people who I'm here to protect." Old Otherwise paused, staring through him. "I'm not here for you, but to protect them, I need to help you. To put a stop to it, you'll need to be forgiven."

"I've asked her for forg—" he said, his throat catching.

"Come on. Spit it out."

He tried to spit it out but couldn't breathe. He doubled over and heaved and heaved, and out of his mouth spilled a thick darkness. Old Otherwise had a hand on his back, and the other helped guide the darkness from his mouth like a midwife. Eventually, it was all out, and he could breathe, and in front of him the darkness took a humanoid shape. It sat cross-legged. It was him. Him before Old Otherwise had elaborated to him the past.

"You already got as much forgiveness as she can give you. This is the one you need next."

He clenched his fists. He wanted to strangle him, wanted to grab him by the back of the neck and grind his face along the ground as the witch house sprinted on its lizard legs. He wanted to turn him into a smear on the world, the smear he'd felt like all these years.

"I—I don't know," he said. "I don't know if I can."

"If you kill him, you will just spit out another until you can."

"Okay," he said, as he leaned forward on his knees to put his hands on his throat and squeeze.

—

After heaving up another, he felt worse.

"I'm sorry," he said to himself, crying again.

"I'm sorry, too," he responded. "We should have looked back sooner."

As the two men embraced and conjoined, Old Otherwise stood up, her old bones creaking in tune to the rotting wood of the house. Out the window was nothing but blue, and he realized that the house had stopped moving.

"Looks like we're here."

"Where?" he asked, having re-ingested himself. He was no longer running from the reality of the pain he'd caused, and the acknowledgment of his faults slowly drew a map for him. "Where were we going?"

Old Otherwise looked over at him, milky eyes turning sharp again. For a moment, she was back in the dress. Barbara.

"We're where you need to be."

He stood up from the floor and looked at Old Otherwise.

"I don't know what to say," he said, turning around to face the door out of the witch house.

"She has to answer the door first."

—

After he'd knocked a few times on the inside of Old Otherwise's door, the door opened an eye-wide crack. Suddenly, it was pouring rain, because it was July and the beginning of the rainy season.

He was standing a few feet from the door, getting soaked. She looked at him, one lens of her glasses hidden behind the door. He was wearing a jacket over a hooded sweatshirt, steel-toed boots, and jeans. He was dressed for the north of Canada, standing in the warm rains of Bangkok.

"What the hell are you wearing all that for?" she asked, opening the door the rest of the way.

"It's a long story," he said. "It starts with me telling you I'm sorry, and then—if you are willing to let me in—telling you why."

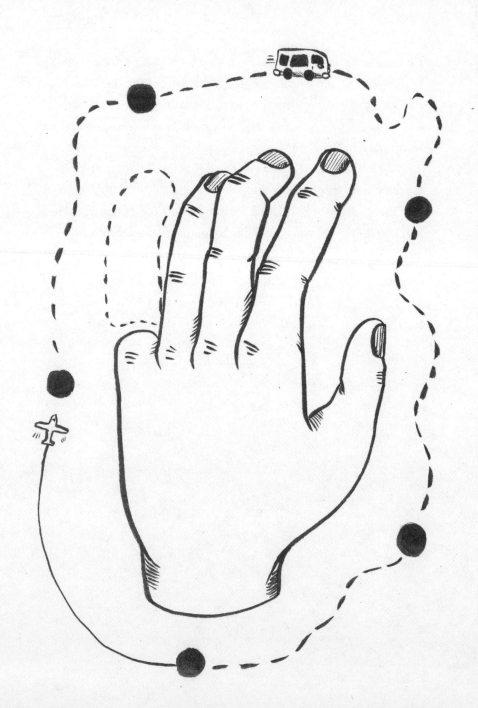

MOVING PARTS

MY LEFT PINKY WAS FIRST. During the icebreaker at my college dorm's first floor meeting, when I was asked to give three interesting facts about myself, I lifted my pinky-less hand.

The first fact was: "I grew up on a farm about five hours away."

The second fact was: "I lost my left pinky finger after I moved in."

And the third fact was: "There's nothing else about me that's interesting."

People nodded. The RA smiled and thanked me. Then, the girl across from me with the pigtails spoke.

———

When Mom picked me up that December for the winter break, I came down with a backpack full of clothes to meet her, the dark-grey family car stark in the snowscape, and I hugged her long and hard until she pushed me away and pulled off my left glove. Then she put it back on.

We didn't talk about it on the drive home, and when I got home and hugged Dad for twice as long, he didn't notice. Not until I was handing boxes of Christmas decorations up to him from the crawl space, plainly favouring my right hand.

He held my left hand and looked at it a while.

—

For my birthday in March, Mom drove down from the farm to buy me dinner. Dad was busy weaning the calves with my little brother. My older brother was supposed to meet us for dinner but an hour before said he was too busy.

Over our bowls of Mongolian stir-fry, Mom handed me a small gift wrapped in blue. Inside was a little finger Dad had carved for me out of tamarack wood, with a strap of leather nailed carefully into the bottom that I could use to secure it onto my hand.

I put it on. The tamarack pinky was the perfect size and shape. Mom smiled at me over our bowls of stir-fry. "He must have used his own finger to scale it," she said.

On the inside edge of it, where I could always see it, he'd carved LOVE, POPS.

—

When summer came and I moved back to the farm, I didn't lose anything. When I went back to school that fall for my second year, to the same dorms but on a brand new floor full of brand new people, I lost my right ear.

My fun fact that year was: "I decided to switch from fine arts, and only after did I lose this ear." The RA laughed and the rest were polite. I sat back down. When the guy to my right talked about himself, I didn't hear a word.

On Christmas morning, Mom gave me the hat with tall elf ears sewn into the sides to wear while we opened gifts. I pulled it down onto my head and stared at myself in the mirror for a long time.

When summer came and I moved back to the farm, I didn't lose anything. I worked the fields, moving cattle for daily grazing, cutting hay for my little brother to rake into swaths that Dad would later bale. At the end of the summer, I got in the car with Mom at six in the morning, and we pulled away. I tilted my chair back and took a nap. I was excited to live in a fancier, quieter dorm that year, sharing a suite with a friend.

When I woke up, we were halfway there, and I didn't have my right foot. My shoe sat empty on the floor.

My suite mate and I didn't bother to go to the floor meeting that year. But if we had, I would have had my script ready: "What I wouldn't give for two left feet."

My gift that Christmas was one heavy woollen sock. For my birthday, a very beautiful shoe.

When summer came yet again and I moved back to the farm, I didn't lose anything. Dad said, "Thank God every tractor clutches on the left," but he didn't let me drive it on the highways between the fields, because I couldn't pair the clutch with the brakes.

At the end of the summer, my older brother moved back to the farm, and my little brother went off to college a whole *flight* away. I wondered if I would ever see him again. That fall, I moved back to the same dorm room with the same suite mate.

But while I was hurriedly crutching down the hall, I slipped and hit my face on a doorknob and broke a tooth.

—

That Christmas, my little brother came back intact. I was shocked. My older brother, on the other hand—after being on the farm a little over four months—had gone completely bald. By the time he moved back to a friend's couch in the city a few months later, his fingernails and toenails had all fallen off.

When summer came back around, I didn't go back to the farm. I moved into a new apartment with my older brother. I had a summer job as a research assistant. When my brother came to pick up my stuff from the dorms, his hair was growing out again. He had eyelashes. His fingernails were halfway to the tips.

When I crutched into his apartment for the first time, I went into the kitchen to get a beer and tried to open the fridge but couldn't reach the handle. I had to crutch a step forward before I could.

The fridge's door had been too far away the first time.

Because I had lost an eye.

—

I worked, and when school kicked off again, I schooled. I was finally living off campus in the apartment with my brother. I had one extra semester to get through to finish my degree. I stretched that semester across a whole year, and because I didn't want to try to start life after, I looked into grad schools. I sat at my computer late into the night, staring at a blank page, tapping my tamarack pinky against the Control key. Over and over until something came.

I applied to schools in far-flung places.

—

By the time the summer came around again and I returned to my research assistant job, I was set to go to grad school almost two thousand miles away, in New York. When I responded to the acceptance, I had trouble breathing. It stayed troublesome for a week, and I went to the ER and they said that I had only one lung, didn't I know?

I didn't know how to answer that question. Because I think that I did know. I think I knew the second before I clicked the mouse button to confirm the acceptance of admission.

—

I packed all I could fit into one checked bag and one carry-on. Some of my friends came over to help us get my things out of the apartment and into my mom's car. We were going to donate the decent furniture I had left to the thrift store before dropping me off at the airport, and she was going to take the extra five boxes of books and my desktop computer back to the farm to be stored for now. I stood at the bottom of the stairs with my crutch in my armpit, breathing, watching my friends carry my bedroom empty.

I couldn't exert myself enough to help. I tapped my wooden pinky on the wall.

I got off the plane at LaGuardia and was given a ride through the airport on a cart. Someone on the airline had probably requested one because they had a passenger with one foot, one eye, one ear, and who had informed the flight staff that if the oxygen got low they would likely pass out due to having only one lung. I sat on the back of the cart and felt away from the world as every exhausted person stared at me sitting on the cart as I zoomed past. As every exhausted person walked through the airport with their exhausted friends. As the driver whistled and beeped his tiny horn. Not even the driver talked to me.

I got in a taxi. I got on a train. I got picked up by another grad student, who made sure to grab my bags and talk very deliberately toward the left side of my head and tried not to stare at my empty eye socket. The less he stared, the more of an outsider I felt. The further away I felt from the way people were seeing me. Before my first class, the assistant director of student life came over to find me in my dorm and asked me how everything was, if I needed anything, told me I could let them know if I ever did. I added their phone number to my contacts as I stood quiet in front of them. Then I sent them a text so they could save my number.

"Please leave me alone thank you."

I had misplaced my tongue.

———

Mom texted me photos of Dad holding fish he'd caught in the river. Of Dad cutting twine off hay bales. Of a bull moose standing in a foggy field whose fence he'd just broken through. Of their new dog with a dead skunk in her mouth.

—

I was not the only graduate student in our program who was missing pieces of themselves. There was a girl with no ribs who came from Arizona and had applied to our program after she'd studied the saxophone for the last fourteen years but had finally stopped getting better. There was also a man with no right leg who still lived in his childhood home with his mother.

I briefly dated the girl from Arizona. We never got to the point where I might open the girdle she kept on her chest to keep her organs in more or less the right place. We did not like the man without the leg. Not because he didn't have a leg. Everyone was nice to him, to her, and to me because of all of these things they saw us lacking in. She and I didn't like him because he kept trying to use the implicit kindness of others to get laid. It sometimes almost worked.

—

What I wrote was picked apart for its connection to what parts of me were missing. Everything I wrote, someone would find a way to tie that in. People would hold doors open for me. People would offer to carry my book bag as I crutched my way into the main building. People would do everything for me if I'd only let them.

Once, I wrote a sonnet that was simply one line repeated fourteen times:

When I imagine myself I don't see who you think you see.
When I imagine myself I don't see who you think you see.
When I imagine myself I don't see who you think you see.
When I imagine myself I don't see who you think you see.
When I imagine myself I don't see who you think you see.
When I imagine myself I don't see who you think you see.
When I imagine myself I don't see who you think you see.
When I imagine myself I don't see who you think you see.
When I imagine myself I don't see who you think you see.
When I imagine myself I don't see who you think you see.
When I imagine myself I don't see who you think you see.
When I imagine myself I don't see who you think you see.
When I imagine myself I don't see who you think you see.
When I imagine myself I don't see who you think you see.

During the workshop, nobody mentioned that it was lazy. Nobody said that the scansion was totally off, that it was neither pentameter nor iambic. They said it was brave, brutal, gorgeous. At the end of the workshop, our instructor took off her glasses, looked at me, hand on her heart, and said, "It is just so heartbreaking how you've made your speaker be missing an eye *inside*."

⸺

The air was so cold on my lung when I landed for Christmas that year. I was exhausted from New York, from dealing with the majority of the students in my workshops.

When I landed, another cart was waiting for me, but I ignored it. It followed after me, the driver beeping his tiny horn, saying that he was there to help me. I dragged my wheelie carry-on bag.

I crutched along. I rode the escalator to where Mom was waiting for me, my brothers standing tall on either side of her. As I got to the bottom, I continued to drag my carry-on myself. They didn't stop me, but as we were leaving, an airport staffer came over and tried to apologize to me for my not understanding that the cart had been called to my gate specifically for me.

When we got to the car, my older brother drove and my younger brother sat in the passenger seat. They were both whole. Mom sat in the back with me.

As we made our way home through the snowy afternoon into the snowy evening, I stared down at my hands. I wanted to sleep, but I was afraid I would lose more of myself. Not at that moment, but later, because I knew that I had no choice but to keep moving. Because I had not yet found the place that had been able to make me whole.

"No matter what," Mom said to me, leaning over the empty seat between us, "there's still enough."

—

When we made it home, after we each got our long hug from Dad, I took off my winter clothes and sat on the couch in the living room. They had finally bought an artificial tree, and it was already decorated. My brothers got beers. They had asked me if I wanted one, but as I tried to say yes, my tongue of course was still gone. I made a graceless noise to them, then looked down again, shaking my head. Then, Dad got up from his chair and left the room.

As my brothers sat down on the couch with me to watch the same old TV shows that were always on, Dad came back with a big wrapped box. He brought it over and put it on my lap.

"I know it's not Christmas yet, but I think this might help you enjoy it."

I looked down at the box. I didn't feel up to taking out my phone and typing up a protest. I tore through the Snoopy-themed paper and lifted the lid from the blank box and gasped. Dad knelt down in front of me and the box and pulled them out for me: my foot, my ear, my tongue, my eye, my lung, and finally my pinky.

He put the foot back on my stub. Told me to turn my head for the ear. Told me to open wide for my tongue. Told me not to move for my eye. Told me to close my eyes and take a deep breath as he stuck the lung up to my lips.

Finally, he undid the straps on the pinky he'd made for me and handed my real pinky back. I put that one on myself.

"Have these been here the whole time?" I asked, looking down at my pinky on my hand and the tamarack pinky in his open palm. "Is this how you got the size right?"

"Yeah," he said, looking down at his tamarack handiwork. "We started to find them sitting on the bed in your old room."

Then, he got up and left and brought out my right foot's shoe.

—

I was whole again. I laughed, I ran after my brothers through the snow, I heard things from either side of me. Depth returned. It felt perfect and right to be able to move fluidly through the world without feeling like I was less, and it felt absolutely wrong because I knew how unsustainable that feeling would've been had I stayed.

"They won't be able to leave here," Dad said, when I was packing my carry-on again, a week after getting there. "They won't go."

"I know," I said. I had already put the crutch beside the door for me to take on my way out. "But I still have to."

"I know," he said, coming up to me and hugging me for a very long time. When he pulled away, he had his shirt held away from his body like a bucket, and all my pieces were there again. With his free hand, he pulled my tamarack pinky out of his pocket and handed it to me.

"But they will always be here for you."

At the end of that school year, I didn't go back to the farm. I went back to the city and lived in the guest bedroom of a friend couple. I was researching once again.

Which was difficult when I had only my left arm. When the summer was over and I went back for my final year of coursework, living off campus this time, I was gone from the belly button down.

I did all the writing I could. I was writing a book about the farm, about growing up there, about the pressure to take it over that I'd grown up under. The pressure to come back and help Dad and the realization I'd had early on that I wouldn't be able to do that. I didn't have what it took. My brothers were better, but they didn't want it. I did want it, I would have, but I knew that everything it would ask of me was too much. I was a coward. My head was clouds. I wasn't the kid built for that. I wasn't the kid he needed.

I had to stay away from the farm to make my work fill that hole.

So when I had to move somewhere, to work and finish my thesis, I chose to move to New York City, by which I mean Jersey City. It was close. I had to try somewhere.

As my friend drove me to my new apartment in Jersey City, with two roommates I did not know—one being a cat—I started to fall apart in the passenger seat. I watched the green of Long Island break off into topography, into deep veins of highways and crushed suburbs. I felt the sky get smaller. The air get tighter. My friend looked over at me and watched as my fingers fell off, one by one, until my hand and my arm and my shoulder too was gone. While my other ear, my other eye, my hair and my ribs and my gut and my spine and my mouth and my nose went. He started screaming at me as soon as he noticed what was happening, trying to get me to stop, like it was some joke. It wasn't all at once—it took a while, it took until we got through the Midtown and Lincoln tunnels and reached my place.

By the time we turned onto my street, I was just a faceless head, nothing much but a weird case for my brain.

By the time he found a place to park, my whole body was gone.

What was left was a pile of clothes and a tamarack pinky. What was left was an invisible cloud of *me*.

———

After my friend carried my bags into the house and told the roommate and their cat that their new roommate was, in fact, there with us, I knew it wasn't the right foot to start a new life on. But he handed the roommate the envelope with all the cheques I'd written for the first few months' rent, as we'd agreed on. So I was set for a bit.

My roommate could not see me, but the cat could. The cat inched close and tried to get me with her claws.

As my friend left, I embraced him, and he jumped at the chill. He couldn't see me. "Thank you," I said. I had to stand half in his bones to speak to him. It was the only way I could get my words to resonate. "You're welcome," he said, then he went back out to his car.

It felt odd to speak after living in my tongueless body for so long. The thrill of it made me want to sit down and spill myself onto the page, which I couldn't do at all now that my body was gone.

The cat followed me around, hissing, until I drifted through the wall into my room.

—

I was floating over a crowd in Manhattan, two weeks later, when I saw her and sank down. She was walking fast with earbuds in, like many commuters, but she was overdressed for the summer. I got in closer and I could see the duct tape around her, just under the clothes.

When she got into the subway, I stood behind the window as the train zoomed along. My non-back getting not-clipped by the tunnel walls. She didn't look up at me, at her reflection, for a while. Then, she did, her eyes meeting mine for a moment. She smiled politely. I smiled too, and waved. Then she half-turned behind her, putting a hand up to her face to either remove the earbud or to adjust her thick dark hair. As she turned, she stopped. Then she turned back slowly and looked at the reflection of herself, and me behind it.

I was seen. She didn't look away for the rest of the ride.

I came into Tiana's life like a cleansing biblical storm. A few weeks after we met, she went to my apartment in Jersey City after work and picked up my bag and my phone and all of my things and moved them back to her place in Brooklyn. I came with her, of course, though nobody could tell I was there but the cat. She hissed at me. Swatted at me. Then I swooped after her and she ran away into my roommate's bedroom. Then we left with all my things.

At night, Tiana would take off her clothes and show me the parts she had duct-taped up. The way she was missing things was different from me. I lost whole pieces at a time, but she had a hole straight through her belly and lacked a three- or four-inch cross-section from the middle of her left thigh. She undid the duct tape on her arms and showed me how she was losing more and more of her arms by the day. Even though she hardly had a bone from her elbow to her wrist, her hands remained and were functional.

"There's something wrong with the way I'm missing things," she said, and I swooped down to her. She looked up at me. Unlike everyone else, Tiana could see me and could hear me without my needing to speak against her bones.

"There's no right way, Tiana," I said. I got closer to her. "Don't believe anything different."

Since I couldn't use my phone or my computer or anything, I couldn't write or call my parents. They would sometimes text me or email me, and I would stand beside Tiana in her apartment in Bed-Stuy and ask her to check my texts, to check my email. When

I asked her to, she would pick up my phone, put in my passcode, and show me.

Mom mostly sent me photos of my body—whole and strong and moving—working on the farm with Dad. In every photo, Dad was beaming or laughing.

"It is just like you are here with him."

"He is happy."

<hr>

Tiana had grown up in that neighbourhood in Brooklyn and had loved it. "But just a few months after I moved back from Poughkeepsie after school, and after I settled into my new job, I looked around at the place and realized: this is where my home should be, but it's not here anymore."

We were walking down the street from the subway toward her place. It was late August by then, and she was holding my hand. I thought about the farm, the photo Mom sent me of her and Dad blowing out the inferno of candles on their shared birthday cake, their birthdays being three days apart. Framed with a blowing, smiling face on either side and reflected in the dark window above the cake: my body, taking the photo, grinning like mad.

I felt a little heavier and squeezed her hand harder, and then a man who was texting and walking bumped into me. I was shocked at the sensation and then he turned around, glanced, frowning but apologizing, then somehow saw me: a naked cloud holding on to a beautiful, short young woman.

He hardly breathed until he started screaming.

<hr>

People began to talk, to leer, to look at me and squint and think they saw me. The closer I got to Tiana, the more visible and physical I started to become. I couldn't go with her to work anymore. I couldn't float around her office. I had to stay in her tiny room in Bed–Stuy.

While she was out, I loomed around the room. I couldn't really touch things, but other people could see me a little, and almost hear me. Every morning, before Tiana left, she would open up my computer to an empty text file and turn on the dictation software. I had to scream into the laptop's microphone to be heard. I would hover there for hours after Tiana left, screaming out all the words that I had been waiting to write, watching the computer try to transcribe them correctly. Words about the farm, about home, where my body was filling a space I was not fit to inhabit. By the time Tiana came back after work, I'd be so depleted that I'd be almost invisible again, but as soon as I heard her coming up the stairs, I would come back. I would be exactly as full as I'd been that morning.

Every night I helped her pull the tape off of her body to allow herself to breathe. Every morning I helped her stuff the missing pieces for structure and put the tape back on.

——

The longer Tiana was in the city, the more she lost. The hole in her belly became a huge oval of lack between her navel and an inch from the top of her sternum. She lost the rest of her arm between her shoulder and wrist. As I started to become more visible with her, it took Tiana more and more time to fix herself up so she'd look total when she walked into the office every day. To make just enough to neither slip into the red nor to pay any more off her student loans than the interest.

I was half-transparent and could no longer float by the time Tiana's head fell off on the crowded walk up from the G train on the commute home. She came back to the apartment with the head under her taped-up arm, the head crying and bruised and dirty. Her hair a tangle. I came to her in the doorway, half-opaque but concrete as I embraced her. Her head cried softly into my belly. The longer I held her, the less and less I could see through myself.

"There's not enough tape in the world," I said.

—

As we left the city with our meagre possessions, heading west in an old clunky Mercury van we bought for $500, I looked over at Tiana. My body would occasionally flicker to half transparency, but it seemed to be back for good. Tiana set her forehead against the window, fogging it up. One hand on either side of her head while her taped body still sat perfectly upright.

"Don't worry," I said, reaching over and putting a hand on her thigh. I could feel the tape beneath, but the spot felt stronger than usual. I poked at her. "Hey."

She pointed her head in her hands to the place on her thigh, then balanced her head carefully on her neck and used one hand to poke the spot. Then, she went to her belly with the other hand. She turned to look at me, and her head did not fall off. I did not flicker.

"I'm all here," she said, grabbing my hand, shaking her hair from side to side. "We're both all here!"

"Duh," I said, continuing to drive toward somewhere new, to a city foreign and fresh to the both of us.

—

When Christmas came, we didn't drive back to New York to see Tiana's family in Brooklyn, but instead we climbed into the old Mercury van and drove north to the farm in Canada. We didn't have much money after our move, but I bought little gifts for my brothers and Dad and Mom. The tamarack pinky was attached to my key ring by then, and I held it while I drove. As we got farther and farther north, Tiana—complete Tiana—watched the world turn into a winter so complete, into a winter unlike any she'd ever seen.

When we parked, it was night. I pulled our bags out of the car, and before we went inside, I said, "I'd like to show you something," then waited, holding her shivering hand. Our eyes began to adjust to the dark.

"Well?"

"Look up," I said, and above us was the Milky Way and all the stars and everything, really. So, so much universe. Then, we heard the front door of the house open, and Dad stood in the doorway.

"'Bout time!" he said. I put an arm around Tiana. Behind him, Mom peeked over his shoulder and waved. "Get inside, it's cold."

As we carried our bags to the door, it opened up again and my body stood there, smiling at us. I could hear my brothers arguing loudly over some ridiculous premise. Life was as it always had been in there, behind the silhouette. It was as good as complete without us.

"Come on in!" my body said, reaching out to grab the bags from our arms and walking into the house with them. And so Tiana and me followed—we went inside together, banging our shoes on the welcome mat to knock off all that snow.

OF ROPES AND ISLANDS

The Other Island

I was born and raised on an island, which was connected to the other island by a very long rope. The rope was probably several kilometres long, and we would drag ourselves across the lake from island to island by means of it. There wasn't much on the other island, mostly just a tall tree, from the top of which you could see the end of the lake, where water became land. Many of us believed that land was a trick of the eye, in the same way a dull, flat rock from far away can appear to shimmer like water when the sun hits it at the right angle. We would climb the tree and marvel at a world we figured we'd never see up close. We didn't go to the other island too often because it took so long to drag ourselves there. We didn't know how to swim, never once thought to flap our arms in the water, because our arms were always clasping onto the rope. Our hands were calluses with five creaky roots.

We didn't even know who had strung the huge rope between the islands; it was one of our axioms. But there was a story we told at night about how the rope was simply a braid of hair from a huge water-breathing beast, humanoid—because every monster in our stories is humanoid—and our island was the crown of its head. The other island we thought was the head of another beast who had the braid of hair in its mouth. This was also the story we used to explain our love rituals. The people of the island, men and women both, would grow their hair out very long, and once it was long enough, and once they were in love, they'd braid it into a kind of rope and offer it to their loved one. If their love was accepted, the other would take the braid of hair in their mouth, and they would sit together and become as close as two islands ever could. If the love wasn't mutual, the one who was offered the braid would simply cut the braid off at the scalp and throw it into the fire so that the one spurned would have to grow the hair out before trying to find love again.

We survived on a diet of fish. We stood waist deep near our shores and stabbed them when they got close.

When the Rope Broke

The rope broke one day when I was on the other island, alone. I had gone there the morning before because I wanted to climb the tree and see the far-off stones on the green horizon, see how distance transformed things. I also wanted to practise braiding my hair in private, because I wanted it to be a surprise when I offered it to my loved one. Most of the time, it's not a surprise. People know it's coming because they get up in the night to pee and see your shadow sitting around the dying fire as you try to braid your hair, cursing to yourself, and when they get back from peeing they always give you away, shaking people awake and pointing. Usually whoever it is you love is aware that you're going to offer them your hair, and they begin to think about whether or not they will take it in their mouth, which is dangerous because it can make someone think too far. People are always up late and cursing, because it is never easy figuring out *how* to braid your hair, especially if you've done it before, because then you feel like you ought to do it differently in order to have more success. There is so much to lose in offering yourself to someone, and only so much hair to grow in one lifetime. I didn't want to screw it up.

When I got to the other island, I climbed the tree and thought about the person I loved, thought about their mouth and their laughter and their quietness and their similarly callused fingers and their long, long hair. From the tree on the other island, I loved them even more than normal, and I looked over at our island from the top of the tree and tried to imagine them on the shore, looking out across the water toward the other island, loving me. I got so excited that I stayed up there all day, and at night I made my braid and slept near the place where the rope attached to the Island. I slept deeply and woke up in a storm.

The lake was rough, but I was so determined, having dreamt of my love, to reach our island. I was strong then, strong in the arms because of how often I pulled myself from island to island, so I went to the rope and pulled myself out and out and out. I thought of my love fretting on the shore, wondering if I would ever return, and that gave me more strength. They were waiting for me, they were circling the rim of their mouth with their finger, waiting for my braid to arrive. But of course it didn't arrive. I dragged myself through the horrible waves and pouring rain only to find myself at the severed end of the rope, in the middle of the water, with no island in sight. The rope that had been the go-between of so many of our beliefs had broken. I was so tired that I didn't think I could pull myself back to the other island, but somehow I did it, dragging myself up the shore.

I realized what all this meant: the monsters who were our islands were no longer in love. Then I slept for what seemed to be days, then woke up and stabbed some fish to eat.

The Braid Is Cut

When I finished eating some fish, I realized that the braid on my head had been undone by the storm, that my hair was a wavy, wild mat. I was sore, and I sat on the shore and watched the rope float back and forth listlessly on the water and I cried a lot. I thought about the time my loved one had given me a very round rock that they'd found on the shore. I thought about the moment when I stabbed two fish at once and they were very impressed, until they stabbed three at once, which in turn impressed me. I even thought about the time I met them halfway across the rope—going in opposite directions—and we shared a smile and a nod. Sitting on the shore alone, I began wondering, unlike the day before, if they were thinking of me at all, whether they were on the other shore crying and waiting for me to pull myself impossibly from the short frayed rope on their end in the same way that I was expecting them to magically appear, tugging on the strands of mine. The rope was so loose that I could tell there wasn't anyone on the other end, but I still sat there to be sure. I sat there for days doing that, only occasionally going and stabbing some fish. I couldn't see the island from the shore, but I could have if I'd climbed the tree. I didn't want to climb the tree because I was afraid of what the distance would look like. I was afraid I would see on the shore, in my mind's eye, my loved one sharing a braid with another, streams of hair going from one's head into the other's mouth.

Instead I found some slightly big rocks and broke them on a bigger rock until I'd created a sharp wedge. I carried it to the shore and cut the remains of the rope, then watched it slowly—far too slowly—pull out into the water and away.

The Calm After the Storm

I stayed alone on the island for a good long while. My hair was growing and growing. I considered doing what widows do when they lose their loved one and sticking my hair into the fire of a torch until it burned down and scarred the roots. Then I wouldn't have any hair at all, ever again. But of course, it is difficult for anyone to give up their hope for love; no matter how many times you circle an island, sobbing in sadness and stabbing fish in rage, there is some small instinct to keep alive the hope that you could find someone who will take your hair in the mouth every night as you sleep, tethered together.

For that calm time after the storm, I walked around the island and, many times, almost climbed the tree but didn't. As much as I wanted to see my loved one, I didn't want to see them. I would get so close to climbing the tree that I would grasp the first branch, feeling the bark more and more as time went on and my calluses peeled away—before running off and continuing to circle the island, philosophizing about love and one person finding another person. In distant exile from my people, I thought that the origin story of what we believed to be an ideal love was kind of problematic, because the islands had only one braid of hair between them. For a few days after realizing this, I walked neck deep into the water, feeling around with my feet to see if there was, in fact, another secret braid below the water. I didn't find anything. I thought of all the people I knew who had found their loved ones like this, with one of them taking the braid in their mouth while the other was free to whistle and bark in the night.

I thought this seemed wrong, as I circled the island—the *other* island, as we always called it—becoming more and more of a mystic, circling closer and closer to the tree that I knew I really wanted to climb as much as I knew it was a bad idea because it would never show me what I wanted to see. But I didn't know what that was anyway.

The Storm After the Calm

One day, I decided that I couldn't handle it anymore, that I had to see the island. I felt weak, I was hungry, so I went to the shores first and tried to find some fish to stab, but it was difficult. Few came close to me, or few were even there. When I finally got one, tearing into it raw in the waist-deep water, I looked up to find a dark sky approaching from the direction of—from my perspective—the "other" island. Another storm.

I scarfed down the fish and ran to the tree in the middle of the island, but by the time I was a third of the way up, the storm was there and the tree was bending back and forth in the winds, and I could barely keep my eyes open to a squint as I climbed. When I got to the top, I couldn't see anything; I was in a great cave of greyness and sound. I didn't know which direction the other island was, as I seemed to be swaying in every direction, and it was very difficult to keep hold. My hair was in my eyes and then it wasn't in my eyes, because the rain was in my eyes, and it only let up when my face got pressed into the bark at the top of the tree. Eventually there was blood in my eyes as well, after that pressing happened for the fourth or fifth time. I could barely hold on. I just imagined—in the middle of that horrible tempest—the other island basked in sun, everyone's hair in everyone's mouths, all of them circling the island in blissful ignorance of my situation.

Then, of course, the tree fell over, which I didn't notice until I woke up the next day, pinned under it and bleeding, near the water where I had once stabbed the fish and where my people would come to visit me.

When the Rope Came Back

I couldn't move out from under the tree because it was too heavy and I was too weak. It didn't seem like the huge tree that it had been when it was broken and on its side, but actually it was almost half as long as the island. I was really impressed, and happy that it wasn't twenty feet longer, or else I would have been pinned beneath the water. My face was caked with blood, and I looked from horizon to horizon to see if there were any more storms coming—because I was afraid—but all I saw were things floating toward me on the waves, and the first thing that floated toward me was the rope that had once been strung between the islands.

There was also a dead fish on the sand beside me, and I ate it while I watched the rope wash in.

My Visitors, and Finally Finding Love

After the rope washed in—which I wasn't happy about, because it reminded me of how far away I was from my people and how I'd learned that love in our culture was a broken concept, something that none but I, who was impossibly far away, knew—the bodies followed. The bodies, of course, were the bodies of my people. At first I was shocked to see them so close after so long and wondered how they'd learned to do that. Before I realized that they were not alive, I thought they'd learned to float in order to find me, that during the time of my exile—which felt like forever—they'd been coming up with this new technique so they'd never need a rope to reach someone again. I cried when I saw them, because after all this time being alone and skeptical about how much they valued me, they'd come to find me. I cried again, of course, when I realized that everybody who was washing up couldn't hear me calling to them, because they were all dead.

I cried, pinned under that tree in the sun, covering my face with my hair. I didn't want to look at them or the bugs that were swarming to inspect them. After a lot of crying, I moved the hair from my face and emerged into twilight. Another dead fish washed up near me and I ate it. I lay there, unable to come to terms with things, with the way I thought a life was supposed to go: you are born, you live, you find love, you live, you die or they die, and you are either sad and scalded bald yet grateful to have had the experience, until you die too, or you are dead and missed. Instead, my life went like this: I was born; I was alive; I fell in love; I was stranded from love; I walked around the place where I was stranded from love, trying to find a way to get back to my love while also discovering that our idea of love is a broken concept; I climbed a tree in a tempest and got no further understanding of the state of my world; I woke up under the tree; I found my people dead in the water and then dead on the shore; and then I died. I didn't get to the last bit right away though. That didn't happen until I decided to take things into my own hands—which could feel so much at that point, because their calluses were nearly gone—for one final gesture.

Through that last night, I braided my hair again and itched at the wounds on my abdomen where the tree was pinning me and where I could smell my flesh turning. The moon was high, and the black forms of my people were lifting and lowering in the waves. I didn't recognize any of them and I didn't try to, because I was past the point where they could do any good for me. They were so close, but further away than ever before. Instead, I tied up my braid, under that full moon, and thought of the story about what happens when someone dies, how their essence turns into a wisp and is carried off in the airstream of the huge birds that fly across the lake once every two seasons. As I tested the knot with my weakening fingers, I wondered what it was going to be like to be carried off toward where the water morphs into land. Would I be able to reach the edge, or would it always stay the same distance away? I didn't know then that you do end up reaching it at some point, it just takes a very long time. Most of the time you're waiting for the birds to come and whisk you away while you're just hovering above the island you died on, looking at all the dead faces that you didn't want to look at when you were still alive, and also looking at your own old face, how peace-less it is but how—being rid of your walls—you are so peaceful now, and so patient. It doesn't take long for you to learn to swoop down and realize what you realized too late: how much you fascinate yourself. You marvel the look of your nostrils, despite their deadness, and you marvel at the small depression where your neck meets your chest. You love the look of all your holes, but mostly—if you are like me—you feel as if you could weep at the sight of your unique repose where you, on that dawn when you finally lost the life you were given and which you did not find satisfying due to it deviating so much from your expectations, you still found a way, in those last moments when your mind was a-stutter with fear and fatigue, to take the braid of your hair in your hand and place it—with firm affection—into your own mouth.

But when you're dead like me, you don't get to weep anymore, because you don't really have the same feelings. And at the end of your time hovering above that island, where your body has melted into bone and where the braid has unhooked from your skull, you're somewhat content with the fact that you wept a lot when you still had the chance. At least, I was. I am.

PATIENT #14

A CANADIAN SCIENTIST, Dr. Lois Rain, discovered a way to manipulate the RNA of the Ebola virus so that, instead of causing a fatal hemorrhagic fever, it would make people grow wings. She developed a special protein that would latch onto several of the largest strains of Ebola and write its own genetic script onto the virus's, resulting in the emergence of wings, which graft themselves to the lower cervical vertebrae and the pelvis—causing, among other things, some stiffness of the lower back. Despite her best efforts, Dr. Rain was unable to develop a protein that grew the wings from the ideal spot, between the scapule, but did succeed in growing them, in subsequent tests, from the ankles, the sternum, and as one single massive wing sprigging from between the eyes (Patient #40, who developed significant brain damage from the wing joint rooting its bone lattice in his frontal lobe and who marked the final variant of the Rain Protein tested before defaulting back to the original). In each of these cases, including the first rear-pelvic placement on Patient #14, the wings were too heavy to practically flap.

Dr. Rain had never intended to cause any kind of physical mutations; they were simply the accidental result of her attempt to stop the virus in its tracks. Of the first cured patient, Patient #14, Dr. Rain noted that twelve hours after administering the protein, he was experiencing a horrible full-body pain. At first she thought his Ebola symptoms had worsened, that there had been a major hemorrhage somewhere in his body. But then she observed that his fever had broken, and she could find no signs of any new hemorrhages in the patient's body. After some preliminary blood tests on the agonized Patient #14, conducted a day after his fever broke, Dr. Rain noticed that the virus seemed to have completely quit attacking his body, despite the fact that the patient rated his amount of pain at all ten fingers—unbearable. She stood over him, fully cloaked in wonder and a hazmat suit, as he squirmed in the straps that held him to the bed as if he were trying to break free of his own skin.

Within the first week, after putting Patient #14 on a morphine regimen to stave off his screaming, Dr. Rain discovered, by means of exploratory X-rays, a calcium buildup in the lower back, just above the buttocks, where Patient #14 was able to direct her as his pain finally localized. Upon inspecting the area more closely with an ultrasound, it seemed that he was sprouting two symmetrical sockets of new limbs. Within two weeks, the huge wings had grown, and Patient #14 was no longer in pain. He was even allowed to walk around the quarantine room, complaining now—though he was still fairly medicated—of a simple constant ache, part of which arose from the nostalgia of growing pains, part from morphine withdrawal, but mostly from Patient #14 hearing the news that his family—wife and children and parents—had recently died of the same virus that had almost taken him.

The first complaint Dr. Rain heard, three weeks after the original widespread "success" of the protein, was that the wings were too heavy and that the surgery required to remove them was very difficult and largely ineffective. The wings had a tendency to return, a tendency to grow into the ridges of the phantom pain caused by their emergence and immediate removal.

On one hand, Ebola was vanquished. But now a new problem replaced it: what to do with all of these winged, grounded people? Patient #14, who had first grown wings (in the preferred place, Patients #16 through #40 being the un-preferred deviants who would have theirs repeatedly surgically removed and Patient #15 getting the protein too late) was the most committed to carrying the wings around. He was a strong man of thirty-two who had, before the epidemic, worked in shipping, but afterward simply wandered the streets of Kenema alone, lifting and lowering his huge, sinuous wings, stirring up loose red dust. He was determined to be mobile, to wander, to pump his wings and try to fly. Unlike many of the patients, who were so weakened by the virus that they were anchored by the huge wings during their recovery, Patient #14 was unable to be still. One day, witnesses caught sight of Patient #14 leaping from a three-storey building and gliding his way to a painful but non-fatal landing, dragging his face along the ground. He got up and walked three-quarters of a mile, face bleeding and wings slowly flexing, before ambulance workers caught up to him.

Once his wounds healed, Patient #14 was moved to a psych ward and put on antidepressants. When he was in hospital, a documentary for *60 Minutes* was produced on the staggering and unlikely accomplishment of Dr. Rain, and Patient #14 was interviewed twice about his experiences with Ebola and the debt he owed Dr. Rain. According to some questionable sources who said they had known Patient #14 before the outbreak, his answers—which, on the whole, praised Rain—sounded as though they were sifted through someone else's brain. This they attributed to his seeming lack of selfness from the effects of the medication, which was sponsored by a family of six in San Angelo, Texas. Within a week after shooting the interviews for *60 Minutes*, Patient #14 disappeared for three days, returning with his body and wings cut up. He was moved to a mental hospital in Freetown where he was kept cooped up for two weeks, reintroduced to his medication, and put on talk therapy and (allegedly) other, more dramatic therapies.

Meanwhile, Liberia and the rest of the Ebola-affected countries in West Africa became aeries of grounded men, women, and children who had been brought back from staring into the brink. Some transgressive media outlets in France dubbed these people "winged corpses." To attempt to help the grounded population, many of the Doctors Without Borders stayed for an extended period of time after administering the Rain Protein and oversaw the wing-sprouting patients, attempting amputations of the heavy wings before they ultimately learned (by the state of Patients #17 through #40, who were beginning to show regrowth) how ineffectual the surgery was. Physical therapists were brought over from the United States to help the people cope with their new, heavy wings, but the problem was that even pre-Ebola, many of the patients were unfit to carry such a weight, especially centred on the cervical vertebrae. A new epidemic had arisen: what to do with a population on its back—not dead, and not dying? How did one cure such stasis? The surviving of Ebola was a whole new unstoppable sickness that left entire countries grieving and dispossessed. Attempts were made to have therapists sent over from North America and Europe to counsel the survivors, but it seemed that no country had enough to spare.

Within three months of the Rain Protein's invention and widespread use, a German doctor—Dr. Lutz Baumann—published a groundbreaking paper (in *Heilung Menschen Quartals*) explaining the reasons why the Rain Protein caused patients to grow large, sinuous wings. This occurred because, in few words, the only known naturally immune carrier of the Ebola virus was the fruit bat. Not only did Dr. Baumann discover this, but knowing this information, he conducted intense—and arguably unethical, if not illegal—experiments in attempts to genetically modify the original strain of Ebola that had caused the sinuous wings to grow when exposed to the protein into a new strain, which he incubated and tested on African swallows. Eventually, after killing an indeterminate number of the birds, he was able to mutate a strain of Ebola that they were immune to but could still carry and spread.

His exciting discovery was that this new manufactured strain of Ebola, when cured by the Rain Protein, caused patients to grow—instead of the sinuous batlike wings—a feathered, lighter variety of wing closer to the swallow's that was more compatible with the average human weight and muscle capacity. He discovered this when he accidentally exposed himself to his new strain and was forced to use the Rain Protein to cure himself. Within two weeks—of agony—Dr. Baumann became the first doctor in all of Europe—in all of the world—who, because of the change in wing density, could fly.

In the fields on the outskirts of cities in Sierra Leone, Liberia, and Guinea, the winged willing were laid in quarantine tents and given the modified strain of Ebola. Two days later, they were given the booster of the Rain Protein. The combination of the two caused another painful metamorphosis, and over the next few nights, thousands of winged men, women, and children screamed and cried as the bones of their wings hollowed out and the sinews pulled back to be replaced by huge, light feathers. Dr. Baumann himself, being the only person known to be immune to the new virus, took charge of the largest readministration program, just outside of Kenema.

Over the next few months, patients began to fly. Many did not bother to learn, afraid of their new anatomies, but many others did. Flocks of the survivors began to be spotted flying along the coast of Tunisia and the Mediterranean. Soon meteorologists began tracking the flocks eastward, through Europe, and daytime talk shows like *The View* discussed the political implications of the survivors finding the airspace over Russia closed to them. One Ebola survivor made headlines when he, by mistake, flew over the Vatican City's no-fly zone, was accused of being Satan spawn, and was jailed indefinitely, until, three weeks later, he was released by means of a papal bull.

They were looking for something, Dr. Baumann said, in a press conference. Dr. Rain, unwilling to be outdone, got interviewed on the BBC and claimed that the winged West Africans were given, by Dr. Baumann's new strain, a simple wont for migration, and were not looking for anything aside from the unconscious satisfaction of their newly constructed biological imperative. She likened the flocks to extinct passenger pigeons, which had been in an almost constant state of migration during the entirety of their lives until they were finally hunted to extinction.

Patient #14 never got these new wings. He disappeared from the mental hospital in Freetown several weeks before the Baumann strain was widely distributed and long before people around the world—largely in poorer war-torn countries—began lining up to be illegally administered Baumann's new strain of Ebola, followed by the Rain Protein, in search of wings. New flocks began to appear in every continent, some hunted down by authorities, and others allowed to fly free. There was a small flock, largely composed of citizens of the southern United States, that was finally trapped in Central Park because they had begun harassing New Yorkers, whom they referred to as "citizens of the ground." Another flock of young tourists in Australia took roost on Uluru with armfuls of goon and marijuana, where they caught flak from Indigenous representatives in the country claiming they were invading sacred land. It was even rumoured that some workers in the Antarctic exposed themselves to the strains in order to give them more mobility in their research of glaciers and ice floes.

Six weeks after escaping the mental hospital and before the world took to the air, Patient #14 was spotted by authorities testing his wings on the docks of Freetown, staring out at the sun as it set over the blank Atlantic. The authorities had been tipped off by a worried boatswain, but when they arrived, their attempts to contain Patient #14 were unsuccessful. As soon as they got within range (they had plans to tranquilize him) Patient #14 spotted them and—despite the weight of his wings—took off into the air, skimming across the calm waters of the Sierra Leone River toward either Kupr or Madina on the opposite shore. The officers on site reported that his appearance was similar to that of a large bat, weak in flight, even going so far as to claim that his face, when he turned toward them, was scrunched in a similar look of permanent rage.

Patient #14 wasn't spotted again for two months, while the rest of the world sprouted their wings and wanderlust. This time, he was spotted by a small scouting flock of the largest flock recorded—consisting of about six thousand people—that had originated in Mongolia. Patient #14 was seen once again on the shores of the Atlantic (this time in Senegal) exercising his wings. Through translators, the scouts claimed that they watched as he "flew out over the ocean with strength equivalent to the moon and with the determination to swallow it."

Patient #14 was next seen by drug smugglers flying west toward the coast of Mexico, winded and weary, around the same time that the Nobel Prize for Medicine was co-awarded to Dr. Rain and Dr. Baumann. Dr. Rain, in her acceptance address, was critical of Baumann for coming along with his controversial strain of Ebola. She accused him of "radically re-aestheticizing [her] landmark cure by unethically manipulating the genome of a dangerous virus that had already ravaged thousands of people, just to see if he could make the survivors more fashionable," as well as accusing him of leaking the strain himself (and to himself) in order to give the world a "new means of existence" that originated with him. Dr. Baumann, his wings modestly folded close to his hips, took his award quietly, claiming in retort that he wanted only to help the people affected by the original Ebola virus by giving them the ability to move freely so that they might find whatever it was that they were looking for.

Patient #14 never found what he was looking for. After flying across the Atlantic and surviving, he flew across the Pacific, and when he failed to find it there, he circumnavigated the globe, from north to south, six times without stopping. Nothing did it. Just as he began his seventh circuit, a flock of the original survivors were flying the coastline of India and the Bay of Bengal—not for fashion and not for fun, but in an earnest search. When they crossed paths, privately and together, they wished that the strain had not only given them each the freedom to look, but the wisdom—or even the courage—to find, or simply to forget the need.

Concurrently, a boy in Visakhapatnam—the largest city of the Indian state of Andhra Pradesh—watched the flock of survivors fly over his city in sunrise. When he heard their voices pass him in the sky, he mistook them for angels singing.

FOUNDATIONS

1

Everything began in the vacant lot out back, which for the year that Lea and Cress had lived in the neighbourhood—one block east of Troost Avenue, in midtown Kansas City—had been nothing but an emptiness chain-linked off and marked by a developer's sign: a promise to one day break ground.

The groundbreaking began with a construction crew cutting down every single tree along the fenceline between the strip of five houses they lived in—two of which were unoccupied—and the vacant lot behind. Lea didn't really pay any attention until her younger Black neighbour rushed over to the site, insisting that the massive tree they'd just felled at the back of his fence had been *his*. That it had been on his property.

He was furious.

Lea was home from work, sitting up in her and Cress's poorly air-conditioned carpeted attic room, and was splitting her time between crudely sketching out some bad ideas for potential sculptures and updating her lesson plans for the sophomore studio course she was teaching that fall at the local art institute where she had once been a student. She came to the little window that looked out over the backyard and the lot behind and saw the huge tree they'd felled two houses over, and her neighbour fuming. She'd been hearing the constant cry of the chainsaws, heard branches snapping against ground and even felt the floor shake as the last massive tree hit the ground, but nothing had been enough to pull her away from her sketchbook. Nothing had pulled her up until she was shaken by notes of human fury.

Her neighbour's big voice carried, bouncing between all the houses on the block, bouncing unimpeded into the now too-open sky. The newly felled tree spread itself across the whole of the lot. She'd never realized how big it really had been until it was splayed out on the ground.

At the window, she also saw how, just like that, there was no more shade on their block. Suddenly, there was a clear view across their postage-stamp backyard, across the vacant lot, to neighbours she'd never seen from their house before. She didn't like the look of their backyard filled with all that undiluted sun.

It felt like an omen, a progression of some sort of machinery— in which she couldn't help but remember that she too played a part—to see her neighbour so irate. To see their other neighbours wandering over to stand near him. To see the workers—white workers—on the lot buzzing, trying not to look anyone in the eye, trying to hurry on with their work.

No more time before to revert to.

2

Some kids grew up playing with fire, but Lea played with lightning. When she was nine, she'd asked her dad to help her build a lightning rod, which they installed at the edge of the potato field across from their house in Williams, Minnesota.

Lea was terrified of thunderstorms, a fear that muted with age but never dissipated completely. Part of her fear came from how lightning felt like God raking the warm coals of the world as if he were trying to reignite it, and the other part came from seeing *The Wizard of Oz* way too many times when she was way too young, because it was her dad's favourite movie. Every time there was a thunderstorm, Lea would sit at the window, staring at the clouds, waiting in horror for the moment when they would begin to turn in on themselves, transforming into a tornado capable of tearing a hole between dimensions. Of turning the sepia into frightening colour. Nowadays, she'd evolved to sitting in bed and petting their trembling terrier, Wyvern, watching *Futurama* on her laptop.

But the lightning rod, crude as it was, had been effective. The farmer who owned the potato field let her dad place the rod—made of rebar wrapped in recycled copper wire—just on the other side of the ditch at the edge of his property and across from their long gravel driveway. It was only six feet tall, but it was the tallest thing for the few hundred yards between the rod and Lea's family's house.

Sometimes, the memory of the morning her dad installed the lightning rod slipped back to her, particularly whenever she was working on a sculpture or whenever else she heard thick metal hitting thick metal. The sound of him driving a two-foot stake of rebar with his mini sledgehammer into the cool soil—the bright ringing being steadily drowned in the muffling earth—lived inside her.

Once the stake was all but completely submerged, she herself had woven the ends of the lightning rod's copper wire through the hole he'd drilled in the top of the stake, giving the lightning a low-resistance path to ground itself. There wasn't much ceremony in finishing the installation; her dad stepped back and stood up taller than the copper-wound iron rod, his gut ballooning as he let out a long breath. There wasn't a cloud in the sky—a stipulation of Lea's that had delayed the installation for four days after he'd finished welding the rebar into the sturdy rod and Lea had finished stripping the salvaged copper wire and winding it along the length of the rod. There wouldn't be a thunderstorm for two more months, and not until she was ten did she see, from her chair at the little window, lightning striking the rod.

Two months after lightning finally struck it, Lea did a presentation on lightning for the science fair at school, earning herself an honourable mention ribbon. Six months after that, she moved to Bemidji with her mom and her older brother, Lars. She wouldn't see her dad—or her lightning rod—for eight more years.

But the feeling of sitting at her window as thunder crashed across the wide, wet world outside—the usual terror still setting in her chest—and seeing, at first, a light sparking around the rod and followed almost immediately by a full stroke of blazing light and energy connecting the heavens to the earth via a conduit of her own design: that had done something irreparable to her.

Eventually, after Lea graduated high school and ran as far away as she could fling herself—to Kansas City, for art school—she would eventually find herself creating work that was haunted by that original rod she and her dad built, making large metal sculptures that reached for the heavens and were similarly created with the idea of conducting lightning in mind—sculptures made specifically to collaborate with the destructive power of thunderheads.

3

A few minutes after Lea watched her neighbour screaming at the workers in the lot, she put Wyvern on his leash to take him for his afternoon walk. It was maybe an hour earlier than usual, but she wanted to go past the site and see what was going on. But as soon as she got outside, she saw police cars at the intersection with Forest Avenue and went west instead. She wasn't exactly sure why. She briefly felt an instinct to go and be a witness in case something went sideways, but at the same time, she imagined the worst-case scenario: being caught in some kind of crossfire. So instead, she walked west across Troost.

As Wyvern was finally circling the edge of Gillham Park, preparing to poop, Lea got a call from Cress. She had stopped at Costco before heading back from a home visit to one of her platonic touch therapy clients north of Kansas City. Cress didn't even say hello when Lea answered the phone; she just said, "Okay, these are the beers they've got," and started listing.

As Lea and Wyvern walked home from the trash can in the park, Lea told Cress about the trees, and their neighbour, and the cops.

"Sounds fucked up," Cress said. "I can't imagine what the energy is like there right now."

"Even I can tell it's bad," Lea said, waiting for a gap in traffic at Troost. Ahead, on their block, there were no more police cars. A good sign, she supposed.

"Well, I'm next up at checkout, so I'll be home soon," Cress said, her voice soft yet tense, as always. "I'll need to borrow those beefy arms of yours when I get there."

"They're all yours," Lea said, her muscles tensing a little as if to remind her that they were there if she needed them, as she and Wyvern stepped out into the street.

4

Long before the vacant lot began to be terraformed by the construction crew, before Cress and Lea moved into the house just off Troost, they had met at a divey gay bar in midtown. Lea was twenty-two at the time, and Cress twenty-seven. Lea was still deep in the shadows of denial about her own sexuality, but she was finishing up her sculpture degree at the art institute, where she of course floated among many queer folks. She'd dated some men here and there and arrived at the idea that perhaps she was asexual. She'd never thought about dating someone who wasn't a man. After meeting Cress, Lea would reflect on her inability to even raise the question to herself as evidence of internalized homophobia, of her subconscious wish to suppress the discovery of her queerness: a Pandora's box best returned to sender.

She'd been at the bar to celebrate her friend Nicky's birthday. Lea had decided to be the designated driver, because lately when intoxicated, she'd been feeling too unmoored, and she went to play some pool to get a breather from the rowdiness of the party. She was a bit tired from the day, having done a lot of welding and metal bending on her senior sculpture final, and she was lining up to break when Cress ambled over from her own little crowd.

"Can I pretend to hit on you for a bit?" asked Cress—tall, black haired, dressed comfortably in a black zippered hoodie over a white scoop-neck tank top, her legs springing exhaustively from a short red tartan skirt—as she reached the edge of the table. Lea blushed and raised an eyebrow. "My friends are a little insufferable tonight, and I used hitting on you as an excuse to get a break."

"Um, sure," Lea said, standing up and holding her cue out to Cress. "If you want a *break* ..."

Cress tilted her head a little at Lea, smiling at the flimsy attempt at a pun. Then she took a step closer and took the cue, as well as Lea's spot at the table. Lea stepped back and stood behind Cress, pressing her back against the wall. As Cress bent over to aim her shot, Lea couldn't help but glance down at Cress's short skirt, which rose to show the lowest edge of her grey panties. Lea looked only for the briefest moment, but her mind eternalized the moment to memory, and then it began to float in the corner of her vision like picture-in-picture, despite the waves of shame that accompanied it.

That moment—its blazing clearness, its resonant thunder—was the closest feeling to her memory of watching lightning strike that rod when she was ten years old. It moved something she would never be able to unmove.

She was so flustered, her heart pounding, that she didn't even notice Cress's cue ball barely grazing the racked balls and scratching in the left corner pocket. Cress cursed, stood up, and turned to Lea with a scowl. "I'm sorry," Lea said, thinking that somehow Cress could tell she'd looked.

"It's fine," Cress said, handing over the cue stick and walking over to the pocket, where she pulled out the scratched cue ball. She leaned over the table, offering the ball, and Lea averted her eyes, reaching out her hand and feeling the cool ball in her palm. Cress continued, "I guess you know now that I'm not a shark." The heat of her fingers grazed Lea's as she pulled her hand away.

5

When Cress finally made it home from Costco on the day the trees fell, she walked out and stood in the middle of their tiny backyard with Wyvern circling her, his little tail wagging, until finally he flopped down in the shade. His tongue fell out of his mouth. Cress and Lea's immediate neighbours were yelling at one another in Spanish, which was not out of the ordinary.

After a few minutes, Cress came back inside, followed by Wyvern, and told Lea she'd determined that the energy was definitely spiking in a very negative direction. Lea, years into their relationship, remained uncertain about Cress's beliefs, specifically how she believed that everything in the world was guided by a web of positive and negative energies. Lea had never fully bought into those beliefs, despite the fact that she'd built a career in constructing sculptures that acted as conduits between the disparate charges of the heavens and the earth.

In the days that followed, work began to speed up in the lot: the tree stumps and their disembodied branches were carried away in long truck beds, and excavators began to dig at the earth. The workers hauled soil out and gravel in and eventually framed out where they would pour the building's foundation.

A man climbed a stepladder to install a solar-powered security camera on a tree between the sidewalk and the avenue—the only remaining tree anywhere near the lot—stationed right above where a porta-potty had been installed. Lea always took the installation of a porta-potty as the surest sign that construction work was getting serious. She'd noted this escalation in some of the other developments around the neighbourhood rushed through by the same developer, each of which had yielded—often in a matter of months after the porta-potty was installed—the ugliest houses she'd ever seen: houses with painted vinyl siding, sporadic windows, and garages as wide as the houses themselves. It seemed to Lea that the company involved had about two or three designs that they reused as often as they could.

One day, Lea had to take a detour on her way home from work, having found the developers blocking Forest Avenue to properly angle their cement trucks. At home, she watched from upstairs as the workers sank tall rods of rebar into drying concrete to stabilize the concrete they would eventually pour for the basement walls. She knew what they were doing because her dad had always worked construction, and she had worked with him many summers while she was an undergrad at the art institute. The workers looked like tiny creatures pressing pins into an oversized pincushion.

It was early September, and the lingering, sweltering summer and its humidity cooked up a storm system west of the city. When Lea got a text with a Severe Thunderstorm Watch for the counties around Kansas City, she was rewatching early seasons of *The Simpsons* on the couch with Wyvern, who was sprawled out asleep beside her, his back leg resting atop her thigh. Lea always felt that this position of his was a kind of tripwire to alarm him should she try to abandon him while he slept. They were alone that night, since Cress was visiting her sister in eastern Oregon that week. The first thing Lea thought about when she saw the text was all that rebar in the mostly dried concrete behind the house. So she got up, waking Wyvern as his little foot fell from her thigh, and went upstairs to the attic room, pulling a little chair—as well as one of Wyvern's many beds—to the window overlooking the backyard.

Wyvern didn't follow her at first, but once thunder began to roll into the city, he suddenly manifested in the bed. Lea put her bare feet into the bed with Wyvern, feeling his breathing, the heat of his body, as she herself grew a little anxious, as always.

In a talk she'd once given at the end of a little two-week artist residency on the east end of Long Island, she made the observation that perhaps she created her lightning sculptures in part to usurp the terror she had felt about thunderstorms while growing up, and to turn that terror instead into excitement. She said that in the talk even though she wasn't sure she believed it, but it sounded as plausible as anything else she could have said. She could have also said, "I make them because they remind me of my dad," but even after all those years, she still couldn't bring herself to think about him much in private, let alone speak about him in public. But the terror—yes, it had transformed over the years, in part because of how thunderstorms gave her the opportunity to test her work. "God's critique," she'd call it, never quite able to pull away from the whimsical belief in some all-powerful being staring down at her from the clouds. She'd never minded too much the feeling of being watched.

That night, though, the work that was being critiqued wasn't hers, so there *was* anxiety. She had images from *The Wizard of Oz* burned into her mind—Dorothy and Toto in sepia, the twister snaking its way to the farm, from the background to the foreground, eventually breaking into and then lifting up the house. She was comforted a little by Wyvern, who, as the thunder began, was sitting directly atop her toes. His warm, wiry fur gave her an alternative sensation to grab hold of. Lea figured that if Dorothy turned out okay in the end thanks to her little black terrier, so might she.

As she leaned forward to console Wyvern, she saw a twinkle out of the corner of her eye and turned her head just in time to see a bolt blast the construction site, transforming the window to a blank white square interrupted by little else but the pincushions of the concrete and rebar stretching into the sky. She couldn't help but yelp, and Wyvern all but jumped into her lap as the thunder's boom shook the house, the neighbourhood, the city.

But inside, at once, she was transported to a time before and a collection of times since—the strike on the lightning rod when she was a kid, awakening her sexuality with Cress—when she had suddenly felt blaringly alive and present. To a place in her body where there was space for nothing but terrific wonder.

6

It wasn't until they'd begun to get carnal—eight weeks after they'd started dating, following that late-night game of pool—that Lea learned Cress was a witch. There were several signs: her bedroom smelled amazing, and there were various pentagrams, excessive candles, and a full-on broom that did not seem suitable for sweeping floors. But most notable was the way during sex she would ask Lea what she wanted them to manifest together. A few times, Cress even drew a tarot card from a deck on her bedside table and placed it between Lea's breasts before she fucked her.

Lea, having never slept with any woman before Cress, thought perhaps these were simply the lesbian quirks she would have to grow accustomed to. She thought that, perhaps, while sex with men was a more stern and spartan, women liked to burn strangely coloured unscented candles, to place various crystals underneath pillows, and to ask their partner to verbalize their "intention" before going down on them.

But after they'd had sex for the fourth time, on New Year's Day, Cress asked Lea if she would like to have her chicken bones read to ring in 2017.

"Chicken bones?" Lea said, eyebrows furrowing in the half-dark.

"Duh," Cress said, slipping off the bed and kneeling to pull a chest out from beneath it. Lea sat up to get a better look at the dark wood, the pentagram painted crudely on its lid, the iron fastenings. Cress picked the chest up. She was blazingly nude, her tattoos snaking around her flexing arms, her breasts resting sweetly on the top of her belly, the thin rings on her nipples glinting in the candlelight.

"Well?" she said, turning toward the living room. "Let's go read them."

So that night, Lea sat cross-legged on the cleared hardwood floor of the living room—the carpet had been rolled up and the couch and coffee table pushed against the walls. She was still naked too and watched as Cress brought out the broom from the bedroom and began sweeping the bad spirits away from the cleared floor, atop which she then drew a circle with handfuls of soil she'd collected from the place where she was raised before she'd left it forever—the Kiamichi Mountains near Honobia, Oklahoma—and kept in a few large Mason jars in the chest. There were red candles lit all around them, which, aside from the street lights angling through the third-floor windows, were all that illuminated the room. The shadows danced as Cress divided the circle into four quadrants with the soil.

She worked with a serene seriousness that made her almost appear possessed. Lea had never seen someone so focused, and it terrified and excited her. Cress pulled from the chest various animal artifacts, including a coyote's skull, a cured chicken foot, and a little steel cauldron filled with the chicken bones. Cress was muttering to herself all the while, words that Lea thought might be Latin, or nonsense, or perhaps simply tongues—Cress had grown up Pentecostal, and later told Lea that that particular practice was the only thing she'd carried away from that world.

Eventually, Cress turned to Lea and scratched her belly with the claws of the chicken foot before asking her to spit on the bones in the cauldron. She placed the coyote's skull in the bottom left quadrant of the circle.

"What do you want to ask the chicken bones?" Cress asked, finally.

Lea's mind went blank at first, then it filled back up with the contents of her small life: her senior sculpture project, a larger-than-life-sized self-portrait built of steel, in which she held her hands above her head as if trying to shield herself from the heavens. She thought about her future—that thing she felt she was shielding herself from—and the letter of acceptance to a grad school out on Long Island that she'd received a week prior.

"Should I ..." Lea started, suddenly feeling as naked as she was. "Should I accept the future that's being offered to me?"

"Good question," Cress said, turning to the circle. "Very cryptic." At this, she swirled the bones in the cauldron—rattling them against the steel—and dumped them into the circle, spilling them across the various quadrants. Lea stared at the scattered bones, not knowing what any of it meant but thirsty for some guidance. While she didn't quite believe in energy like Cress did, she could not keep herself from believing in the ritual of magic. Cress stood closer, inspecting where things had landed. Lea couldn't help but be transfixed by Cress's hanging breasts moving softly below her as she surveyed the bones as if they were dowsing rods sensing an underground river.

Cress pointed. "Okay, these bones here—the rib and the wishbone—they are crossing in a *T* shape, which means that there's a sort of blockage between them. Perhaps your dreams are struggling, or perhaps the future will be a struggle." She indicated another quadrant, which the coyote's skull was pointing toward. "This wing and thigh"—she bent closer to the bones, her right breast resting softly atop the skull—"I think it's a thigh? Yeah, it is."

She sat back up and looked back over to Lea, who shifted her eyes back to look Cress in the face. "This maybe means there's some sort of guide, or some kind of message from your ancestors. Maybe you just have to listen for that sign, or realize that you've been given it."

"What's this one?" Lea said, pointing to a bone in the middle of the cross.

"That's the breastbone," Cress said, sitting back and glancing openly over at Lea's smaller chest and smiling. The almost childish way Lea and Cress objectified one another was one of the most invigorating parts of their relationship. "That bone is all about things like love, or passion. Since it's in the middle of the cross, it is probably the thing you need to centre when you decide how to interpret the wisdom of the bones."

7

Troost Avenue is a historic redline in Kansas City where race and class have been divided for a century. Lea, never having lived in any other city—Bemidji didn't count—hadn't realized just how segregated Kansas City was until she was told. She'd lived in the city for nearly a decade before she learned anything about J.C. Nichols's racial housing covenants, birthed to help keep neighbourhoods "pure." But once she was told about them, and that the population wasn't quite as white as she'd perceived it to be, she began to realize just how white the city felt.

All Lea had ever known about Troost was that she should steer clear of it, because the avenue marked the place where the "good" part of town became the "bad" part of town. She'd never really questioned that belief, because she hadn't ever needed to go east of Troost. She didn't butt up against her conceptions of Troost until she and Cress—as the pandemic began to fall into static—started looking to move into a place bigger than their tiny one bedroom in Hyde Park. The problem was that they didn't have a very large budget, so the only places they could afford were either just east of Troost or in farther-flung neighbourhoods that were as white as Kansas City wanted you to believe that it was. Lea had been out of town, doing the two-week residency on Long Island, when Cress looked at the place by Troost.

Cress sent Lea photos and videos and described the place over the phone. "It's really cute, and huge! It has a nice energy, very chill."

"What about the location?" Lea asked, pacing her small studio's dark hardwood floor. It was scattered with her sketches, which she navigated in her bare feet as though they were shards of glass.

"It's not so bad. There're some coffee shops close by. It seems to just be a little residential neighbourhood. I saw some dogs too. I'm sure Wyvern will enjoy barking his brains out there."

By the time Lea got back to Kansas City, she and Cress had already e-signed the lease, and they packed their little apartment and moved in, with the help of a few U-Hauls and half a dozen lesbians. The house was huge, as promised, and it was cute—though its cuteness would feel less novel when Lea discovered the miscalculation of their budget due to the increased costs of utilities.

But it was a nice neighbourhood, once the nearby urban decay along Troost fell harmlessly into the background of their life, though Lea couldn't shake the guilt that they were contributing to the creeping gentrification of the area. In fact, they were almost too broke to afford their place, but she knew, deep down, this was how it always started.

Worse, to her, were the development signs in the surrounding blocks, which, over the year they lived there, each began sprouting their own ugly new-build houses with price tags of nearly half a million dollars—twice the average of the other houses in the neighbourhood.

And even worse than that was seeing people actually buy and move into those houses. Lea figured that more and more people actually paying those prices—especially for *those* houses—meant property values would increase. With property values increasing, so would property taxes, which would eventually push the working-class folks out of the neighbourhood. It was a sign that the plodding machine of gentrification was staunchly in motion.

8

After the lightning strike on the construction site, the storm didn't stick around long. Like many of the most snorting of thunderstorms Lea had met in her life, it was climactic but not prolonged. Once the thunder began to clearly resonate from the east and the rain became melodic, Lea got up from her observation chair, went downstairs, and smeared some cheap peanut butter on a lick mat and put it down for Wyvern as a sort of peace offering for not taking up their usual ritual of hiding away in the bedroom during a storm. Lea sat beside him on the cold tile floor of the kitchen, petting him, even though he sometimes growled lightly at her, thinking she was going to take the mat away from him. As they sat together, Cress texted to say she was going to bed along with a heart emoji. Lea sent one back.

Lea brushed her teeth and got into her pyjamas, but couldn't bring herself to go to bed right away, so she went upstairs and sat in the chair by the window again. She couldn't see anything out back, but she felt like something had shifted. Something unfinished was there, or else something was beginning, and she even thought she heard a gentle but steady tone coming from the site, as if the struck rebar was softly singing—but she decided the tone was a trick of her ears, still recovering from the thunder of the strike. After staring at the dark for about an hour, which felt like only about fifteen minutes, Lea went back downstairs and slid into bed, where she faced a night of blazing, indecipherable dreams.

The next morning, as she refreshed herself on the readings she'd assigned to her sophomore sculpture students—which she knew most of her students would not read—she heard voices in the lot and went back up to her window, angling the venetian blinds so that she wouldn't be very visible if someone were to look in her direction. A crew of four workers in yellow hard hats—and a fifth with a white one—and reflective vests were looking at the site, particularly at one section where, Lea assumed, the lightning had struck. They looked concerned, or annoyed. She couldn't see from her vantage point what the strike had done to the concrete of the foundation. The workers talked and gave particular attention to the man in the white hard hat. He had hairy arms and thick glasses and chewed on his lower lip as he knelt at the spot, stood up, scowled, then shrugged. He lifted a hand and drew a circle with his finger, a gesture that seemed designed to give more impact to his decision to keep working, despite the fact that the strike had likely done damage to the foundation.

Halfway through her meeting with her small class of sculpture students that afternoon, Lea abruptly ended their discussion of the readings—whose conversation was mostly sustained by her, the creative writing double major, and her one particularly theory-based student—and told them to work on their projects for the rest of class. The students looked at each other as Lea excused herself, some of them perhaps thinking, it occurred to her, that they'd offended her by not doing the readings. She went into the bathroom, slipped into a stall, and put her face in her hands as her body was racked with deep, thick sobs. She eventually settled, reset herself, and tried to imagine that everything was fine, that this was just a strange sideways release of some unconscionable energy. The stress of being an adjunct at an art college, perhaps. Or perhaps she missed Cress, who had been gone for five days. That thought did succeed in tightening her up, strengthening her facade, because it was followed by the realization that she did not actually miss Cress at all.

In the mirror, she saw that her face was a horror, hideous in its puffy redness. After splashing some water on her face in a vain attempt to return it to its usual steeliness, one of her students, Harper, wandered into the bathroom.

"Oh," she said, expertly painted eyes widening under her bright-green bangs as she made eye contact with Lea in the mirror. She was wearing a surgical mask, as some students had elected to keep up that practice. "Is everything okay, Professor Jensen?"

Lea couldn't help but laugh at being addressed so profession-ally, which probably didn't help matters. Finally, she responded, "Yeah, I'm okay, but I think I should go home. Can you tell the others to either stick around and work in studio, or they can take the rest of the afternoon off?"

At home, Lea walked Wyvern, avoiding the construction site on Forest. She walked west, crossing Troost and entering that charming and clearly more affluent—and white—neighbourhood, passing the string of mansions that were rented out on Airbnb and where football fans from away teams often stayed. People who could afford both to travel and to attend football games.

Wyvern was happy to see her, and his tongue flopping out the side of his mouth—a side effect of having had a few teeth extracted earlier that year—as he ambled down the streets helped Lea feel less untethered from her feelings. More grounded. She had only left him alone for a few hours, but she was so happy to come back to him again, to his little front paws slapping her on the thighs when she walked in the door—mad at her for leaving, adoring her for returning.

When they made it home from their walk, Lea decided to be irresponsible and ordered a pizza. She ordered it from a third-party app, since most of the pizza joints that had their own delivery services excluded anywhere even half a block east of Troost from their delivery area. After she ordered, using the account she and Cress shared, Cress sent her a text with a screenshot of the order notification: "Enjoying your time without me, I see ;)"

As Lea reacted to the text with the cry-laugh emoji, she began to hear the soft tone of the night before, of the rebar singing, and the white hard-hatted man walked into her mind. Then the man opened his mouth, and then out of his mouth climbed another man who looked very similar to him: also hairy, also tall, also wearing glasses and a white hard hat, only his hat had doodles in permanent marker all over it—doodles done by a child who would one day become the artist she always somehow was.

The man, of course, was her dad.

9

Two weeks after she had her chicken bones read by Cress, Lea accepted a spot in the MFA in Visual Art program on Long Island, and a week later—after she finally told Cress that she was going to move out to New York in the summer and would be gone for three years—she and Cress broke up.

Cress, who had herself been positioning their relationship as something casual and fun, knowing that it was exploratory for Lea, got surprisingly upset when Lea told her the news.

"And you were just going to leave me here?" Cress said, through her teeth. "You weren't going to ask me to come with you?"

Lea wasn't sure what to say, because she wasn't sure what she felt.

"I think some time away could help me move through all of this," Lea said, eyes beginning to mist. She didn't want Cress to stay in Kansas City either, but she had never asked anyone to be a part of her future before and was terrified of how that might tether them together in a way neither was actually prepared for. "We don't have to break up or anything, not exactly."

"The fuck we don't," Cress said, turning away from Lea and heading to the door. "We just did," she said, as she slammed the door behind her.

Heartbroken, Lea began swiftly falling behind in her classes. She kept texting and calling Cress, trying to get her to talk again, not wanting to leave things as they had. Eventually, she turned to their mutual friends, and particularly her friend Castro, who, out of all the queers Lea had met through Cress, had installed themselves most firmly at her side. Castro texted her: "I bet she's just real sensitive bc of the whole divorce shit she's been going through."

"Divorce?" Lea asked, feeling a dark vessel opening up to her, filled with a fury of her own.

"OH SHIT. Did she not tell you about that?! That's wack."

Lea didn't reply to Castro but called Cress once more. To her surprise, Cress picked up, and Lea opened her mouth, then hung up. The shapes in her body—grief, fear, fury—shifted, rubbing up against one another, building a static charge. She waited until three in the morning, when she felt sure that Cress wouldn't pick up, and left her a voice mail. Spilling all the things she felt.

In some ways, being given permission to be angry helped her reallocate more energy to finishing her last semester as a senior. Cress tried to call her a few times in the following weeks, but Lea didn't answer and didn't listen to any of the voice mails. She and Castro spent Valentine's Day together, drinking and cursing the heart, giving Lea a hangover that kept her from attending any classes on the busy Wednesday that followed.

In mid-March, Lea's dad called her—a thing neither he nor she was very good at doing—and she told him that she'd gotten into graduate school in New York.

"New York *state*, I should say."

"Hey squid, that's great. I'm happy to hear that." She couldn't tell if he was drunk. "Are you still coming home to work for the summer? Could use the help."

"I don't think I can. I'm thinking of just moving out there at the start of the summer, since it'll probably be easier to get on a lease that isn't bloated for the school year. Could be easier to get a job too."

"That's not a bad plan," he said, followed by a brief pause. "I could give you a raise though? Johnson seems like he's maybe going to move on soon. And there's a few big projects that I could use someone with actual talent on."

"I don't think so. Sorry, Dad," Lea said, looking out the window of her little bedroom, hearing the sounds of her roommates playing *Mario Kart* in the living room.

"It's okay, squid."

"Are you still coming down for the senior show?"

"Hoping to," he said.

When the senior show approached, her dad finally called and said that Johnson had quit, like he'd feared, and he was looking hard for his replacement. Some deadlines were passing, and some patience thinning. He said he'd started waking up in the middle of the night with his heart pounding.

"I promise you, squid, I'd much rather be there. It kills me not to."

Three weeks after that conversation, after Lea drove across the country to move into a little basement apartment in Port Jefferson, New York, she got a call from her brother, Lars, who was the only family who had made it to Kansas City for the show—not that her mother had been invited. Lars had also left home as soon as he could, moving in with some of his friends locally in Bemidji, where he lived until Lea finished high school and moved to Kansas City. After Lea left, Lars signed up for the Air Force and became a mechanic. He worked on drones. At that point, he was stationed in South Dakota.

"Lea," he said, when she picked up. His voice sounded like it was being pressed through a mouthful of nails. "It's about dad."

Lea grew acquainted with public transit that week, taking the Long Island Rail Road from Port Jefferson to Woodside, then a bus to LaGuardia. Lars picked her up in Minneapolis, and they drove north to Williams together. It didn't take them too long to get everything sorted out. The most awkward thing to manage was their dad's business; his clients were, of course, as understanding as possible. Lars took that work on, and Lea cleared out their father's little house, deciding what to hold on to and what to sell.

He'd left no plans, so they decided to cremate him.

"Where should we scatter him?" Lars asked Lea, when they received the little box of ashes from the funeral home. Lea didn't have an answer; she realized she'd never had a chance to get to know her father well enough to know where had felt special to him. The only place that came to mind was under the little lightning rod she and he had built, shortly before their lives changed forever.

10

When Cress got back home from Oregon, Lea didn't tell her about the strike on the site's foundation, or her breakdown at work. Lea and Wyvern picked her up from the airport, and after a kiss, they drove back to their little house as Cress talked about her sister's new baby, as well as the view from her little house on the outskirts of Union.

"Something to be said about living in a place where you can look out on more than anti-abortion billboards from your front porch," Cress said. Wyvern, with his hind legs on the back seat, stretched forward to put his front paws on the console between them and stared out the windshield. Lea gave the side of his face a scratch. "Though I'll say, eastern Oregon also felt more conservative than southeast Oklahoma. I didn't tell Morrigan that I thought she might like living there because it shares some of the nicest qualities of *home*."

Back at the house, Cress gave Wyvern a walk, and Lea carried Cress's luggage inside and started making dinner. When Cress and Wyvern returned, Lea expected Cress to talk about the shift in energy. Lea herself had felt a kind of gravity coming off the site, as well as still occasionally hearing that phantom tone. She had expected Cress to be bowled over by it. But instead, Cress walked into the kitchen—after Wyvern had sprinted all throughout the house upon their return, looking for Lea, who was very obviously in the kitchen—cupped Lea's tiny buttocks as she was chopping up chicken sausages, and asked, "What's cookin'?"

Lea began to wonder if maybe she'd dreamt it all: the strike, the tone, the men detecting the problem in the foundation and then deciding to keep working despite it all. In the weeks that followed, the workers installed the frames and then poured the cement for the walls to match the tall lengths of rebar. They trimmed the tops and began pouring the concrete floor of the basement. Everything was continuing as if nothing had gone wrong. Loads and loads of rock moved in and out. Or, perhaps, like Dorothy, the storm had carried Lea into some new reality, where everything was wrong.

All the while, Lea kept working with her students. In the downtime during studio, while her students were working independently, or when she was at home on the couch with Cress and Wyvern, as either sitcoms or soap operas droned through the TV, Leah often found herself staring at her sketchbook, trying to devise a project to pour herself into. Nothing worthwhile had come for a long time, and it worried her. She hadn't gone through so long a dry spell in a while.

Sometimes, when she went up to the attic room—to get something from the closet, or to do her kettlebell workouts when she didn't have it in her to make it to the gym—she would look out the window for a long minute, staring at the site. Even weeks after the lightning strike, she felt its energy palpably; at first it had felt wispy and bright, then it began to feel more solid and murky. It was hard to explain, and she would have tried to explain it to Cress, but she wanted Cress to feel it herself. To corroborate Lea's feelings. Lea would stop and stare, transfixed, before finally pulling herself away from the window.

After midterm critiques came and went, the news zoomed in on an explosive moment in the conflict between Israelis and Palestinians in Gaza. Social media swarmed with hot takes, where almost every institution in the US took the side of the Zionists rather than sympathizing with the subjugated, colonized population. Videos upon videos of the bombardment of Gaza filled every newsfeed Lea swiped on, and so she was confronted with yet another system of racial conflict that she was complicit in, insofar as she paid taxes to arm the state that held the Palestinians in their open-air prison. Yet another code set to justify colonial forces spreading like a bulldozing rot over stolen land.

It wasn't until the escalation of this conflict that Cress talked of any big shift in energy. But what Cress described—an energy not unlike electrified fog snaking over the whole of the country—was nothing like what Lea had been feeling. Lea felt as though each of her neurons was slowly being hooked into some dark matrix.

One night in late October, as the weather was chilling, Lea got up out of bed. She hadn't been able to sleep. She'd felt agitated, and embarrassingly aroused, but Cress—as had become the norm in the last few years—had lost her ability to detect such things. The polarity of their sexual magnetism seemed to have shifted. It was like Lea had slipped into a kind of Faraday cage her energy was unable to escape from, whereas earlier in their relationship— before they'd broken up for the first time—their magnetism was strong and straightforward. She slipped out of the bedroom, closed the door quietly on Cress and Wyvern, and walked up the creaky stairs to the attic.

Moon and street light spilled into the room from the windows at either end. Lea found a spot just out of reach of the light and crawled face down onto the floor, her cheek rubbing against the carpet as she lay atop her cool hands. Her mind was an exhausted misfire of static as she fucked herself, thinking of no other body in particular, no other hands. Instead, she simply reached out, in her mind, toward the blasts of oxytocin and dopamine she hoped would arrive with her orgasm to wash her mind out. When the orgasm came, it almost brought hope on its back, but as always, it was never quite enough.

She sat in the dark for a while, feeling gloomy but refreshingly untethered for the first time in months. As she walked back to the stairs to finish her night's sleep on the couch, she looked out the back window at the construction site she'd been studiously avoiding for the past few weeks, whose pull felt surprisingly weak at that moment. Before looking out the window, she thought that perhaps she was a few good fucks away from freedom. That all she really needed to fix everything that seemed to be leaking in her life was for Cress to begin to take a hint.

But once she looked out the window, she forgot that she'd ever thought such a thing, because, in the street light, she could no longer see the concrete walls of the site, or the piles of stone, or the wood frames where the floor would soon be lain. There was just a shadowy impression of the place where it all once sat.

11

It was a Thursday night in early June. Lea had been sitting in her little apartment in Port Jefferson, New York, falling into a YouTube hole while applying for jobs, while at the same time, Lea and Lars's dad was drinking at the tavern up on Lake of the Woods. He drank there for a while, acting no sadder than he usually did, according to the bartender, and then he left. The bartender didn't remember how many beers he'd had.

"I don't count them, I just pour," she told Lars, when he went asking.

Their dad had always driven drunk, and it was mostly just fifteen miles of back roads from the tavern to his place. He'd done it a million times—why was this one special? He made it home. He was driving his work truck, which probably meant he'd been on site, working on a cabin near Zippel Bay, and hadn't bothered going back home to swap to his little sedan to go out drinking. He wasn't afraid of anyone stealing his tools from his truck parked outside the tavern.

When he got home, he opened the garage door and drove the truck inside. Then, he closed the garage door.

There was no real investigation. He didn't show up to site the next morning, and after not being able to reach him on the phone, his new employee drove over to check on him. When the employee got to the house, he could hear the truck running in the detached garage, but the garage door was closed. He went to the window on the side door and looked in. The headlights lit the garage. Their father was slumped over the steering wheel.

Paramedics and firefighters declared him dead when they eventually made it there. It wasn't clear exactly what had happened, but because he'd been drinking, they assumed he'd passed out as soon as he got home. "Bad timing."

Lea wished that Lars had let that go when they heard the story from their dad's employee.

"I'm not sure," Lars said. "The truck was *running*. If he got home even an hour after leaving the tavern—which closed at eleven—I don't think there's any way the truck could keep running from midnight to, like, eight a.m. The same carbon monoxide would have choked the engine out by then."

Despite Lars's theory, they never got any sense of what their father had done. Perhaps he'd passed out in the truck and then woken up and turned the truck back on, then passed out again. Or maybe he had gone out again and drank by himself on site or on the lake. Those hours were lost, and they would always be lost.

The thing that shook Lea the most about those hours was knowing that, if Lars was right, and the truck wouldn't have lasted so long in the closed garage, her father might have sobered up by the time he closed that garage door and turned his truck on. That since his employee was surprised he wasn't on the site at 7:30 as planned, he was clearly too functional an alcoholic to still be so out of it several hours later.

But they would never know anything, really. There was no note, no sense that anything had been particularly different. All Lea could conclude was this: "If I'd been here, working with him, I would have been sitting right beside him in that tavern. I would have driven him home and made sure he made it to bed."

12

After Lea saw that the unfinished house out back had disappeared, her first thought was that perhaps the orgasm had succeeded in washing her mind out. That perhaps there never had been a house being built on that lot, and her mind had simply created the last few months of her life in the moments since the orgasm left a vacuum in the razed ground of her mind. But then, of course, she surrendered herself to a more depressing truth: this life was hers, and she was inside of it.

But of course, this truth didn't explain anything.

It was a little after midnight by the time she quietly went down the stairs, double-checked that the bedroom door was closed, and went to the front door. She put a long coat on over her pyjamas and put her phone in one pocket and her keys—and mace—in the other. She instinctively reached for Wyvern's leash before stopping herself. She would have to be her own Toto. She disengaged the security system and opened the door.

She wasn't sure what she expected to see that might explain the absence. Perhaps it was all just some trick of the darkness paired with the creepiness of Halloween looming. Perhaps the street lights on Forest—which were admittedly weak and a fair distance from the lot—could not be trusted.

The night was cool and empty. Now that the fall was officially chilling the city—a salve after the brutality of the Missouri summer—the nights were no longer filled with the screeching call of crickets and cicadas. She rubbed the plastic casing of the mace in her pocket as she turned down Forest Avenue toward the site.

Somehow, she believed her eyes less when she was on the same level as the site. As she walked toward the lot, she could see that the porta-potty was still there, beside the sidewalk, as was the solar panel for the security camera that was nailed onto the tree. The camera itself had gone missing a few days after the man climbed the stepladder to install it—a sign that there was much shadowy protest of the building emerging there.

She wasn't sure what she expected, but once she got to the lot, she turned on the flashlight of her cellphone, just to be certain. She even took a photo, which barely looked like anything because there was nothing there but wet, bare earth where someone might be preparing to frame and pour a foundation.

Nothing was there but the dark. The draw she had felt to the place was missing too. She felt, suddenly, that she wanted to leave. She wanted to walk back south on Forest toward her own street. But when she did, she found herself continuing past her intersection, going farther south on Forest. The night was quiet, but she heard some crunching down the avenue, saw shadows dancing between the trees that lined the street. No dogs barked at her, no windows were lit. A few red eyes loomed from Halloween decorations hanging from her neighbours' stoops. The occasional security light flickered on. As she walked, the sound grew louder, and when she reached its origin, she found precisely what her body had known she would find: the unfinished building, hulking on a lawn in the dark, feasting upon an old house.

The unfinished building had reshaped itself, breaking its concrete walls and floors into legs and teeth, shifting its rebar into ligaments, and separating its wood joists into a torso, some arms, and long fingers—which were peeling strips of worn shingles and rotten siding from the house and dropping it all into its mouth. Lea stood there, maybe twenty feet away, watching as the building tore apart its kin, slowly putting piece after piece between its concrete jaws and crunching, swallowing the pieces to some bottomless gut she couldn't fathom. As it ate, the building hummed that same singing tone Lea had been hearing off and on since the lightning struck the foundation. She stood there long enough for her teeth to chatter and to see the old house be eaten, from the roof to the ground floor. She pulled out her phone and saw that it was nearly three a.m.

Lea woke up on the couch the next morning to Wyvern climbing up atop her—furious that she had abandoned him in the night. The first thing she tried to do was check her phone, but the battery was dead. So Lea got up, went to the bedroom to plug her phone in, and walked into the kitchen.

"You're quite the fright this morning," Cress said, putting a hand out to tickle Lea's side as her other plunged the French press. "Did you get any sleep?"

"Not really," Lea responded, passing Cress to open the back door. When she opened it, the security system did not begin its countdown to alarm, and she recalled disengaging it the night before. Impossible images began to surface in her brain as Wyvern sprinted out to the lawn to pee, and over the tall back fence, Lea saw three workers putting plywood floors down on the joists of the building in the lot behind the house. She stared as Wyvern came up the stairs and looked up at her, until Cress came out the door behind her. Wyvern bolted past Lea into the house, and Cress held out a cup of hot coffee. Nail guns punctuated the morning.

"Really making some progress back there," Cress said, as the coffee burned the roof of Lea's mouth.

13

Lea couldn't help but slip into debt the summer of 2017, after making it back to Port Jefferson following two weeks in Williams and ghosting every interview request for the jobs she'd been applying to. She couldn't bring herself to try again. She did spend a lot of time dealing with some of the estate stuff from afar. She didn't leave her little basement apartment much, and most days didn't talk to anyone but bankers and insurance or real estate agents. She didn't talk to anyone who might ask her how she was, but everyone she did talk to—strangers who were dealing in the business of her dad's death—still offered her their condolences. She and Lars did talk a few times a week, but while they stalked around their triggers—keeping tabs on their locations—they never struck them. They weren't really that close for siblings, though they were as close as anyone in their family ever got. But dealing with their dad's estate drove them further apart.

The debt Lea accrued over that summer dissolved as the semester began and their dad's piddling life insurance money was split between them. Having been self-employed, his policy was about as cheap as he could get away with paying for, at $100,000, which the two split down the middle—though Lars had told Lea to take three-quarters to help pay for her out-of-state tuition. Lea would have done it, but something inside her made her think that if she took three-quarters of the estate, she would be burdened with three-quarters of the responsibility to remember him and to honour his life. Or that she would take three-quarters of the responsibility for his death, accidental or not. That he would have been three-quarters her dad and only one-quarter Lars's. These were the sorts of unspoken, unacknowledged problems that began to sew distance between her and her brother.

Lea was dissociating that first semester, trying to pretend she was still capable of art. She found excuses to skip social events, complaining of work shifts that didn't exist. Eventually, she got tired of having to juggle all of her fake excuses and finally got a real job with bad hours as a server at a bar and grill on the harbour, a few blocks away from the ferry port. She was the least bodacious of the servers at the grill, but she was able to hide behind the false face manifested by her deep desire to not be herself: a bubbly, short, curveless creature that would wink after taking any order.

One night she stepped outside to take her fifteen and saw a text from Castro asking her how she was doing. It was the first time anyone she'd known in Kansas City reached out to her in any sort of real way, though she of course hadn't told anyone anything about her dad and had long since deleted all of her personal social media accounts, leaving only a few for art. As she looked down at the text, the salt smell of the Sound mixing with the steamy miasma of the bar, she imagined Castro sitting in the corner of some social gathering where they knew everyone but didn't want to talk to any of them, realizing that Lea was missing from their life. This was clearly a fantasy, but Lea believed in it. She wanted nothing but for it to be true. She felt her chest tighten. She lost her hold on the air.

"My dad killed himself this summer," she typed, sending it before she could consider stopping herself. She followed up with: "Now I'm trying to trick drunk straight Long Islanders to give me better tips."

"Oh fuck, Lea," they replied, very swiftly. "That's fucked up!"

"Yeah, it is fucked up," Lea texted, realizing in that moment that it really, truly was.

Castro and Lea started texting a bit more after that, and eventually Castro even convinced Lea to look into counselling services at her university. It turned out there was a clinical psychology master's program that offered therapy sessions from graduate students for twenty dollars a session to current students. The program was housed in one of the many buildings on campus designed by an architect who had mainly designed prisons, which meant it had thin hallways and few spaces where people could crowd. Lea sat in a chair in one of several little offices once a week and talked to a woman named Eleanor, who often annoyed the shit out of Lea but who helped get her head a bit less tangled. Eleanor would identify and cut off Lea's "mind-reading" tendencies. It pissed Lea off to be challenged like this, but every time Lea left a particularly prickly session promising herself she would never return, she would wake up the next morning feeling the effects of what Eleanor was doing.

As the semester's end neared, Lea started getting her act together in her classes a bit more and realized just how lonely she was. She'd been so distracted by grief that she'd never stopped to look at how quiet and sad her life had become—how it had been that way for a long time. She started going to class and realized that she had become the odd one out, that she was the one nobody really knew. On Thanksgiving, after eating cold leftovers on her bed, she texted Lars, wishing him a happy Thanksgiving, but he didn't text her back for three days.

On the last day of the semester, after saying goodbye to her classmates, she slipped out of the end-of-semester get-together and drove back to her apartment. Walking in, she felt the immense weight of her life. She wanted anything, anyone—a sign. She thought about texting Eleanor but didn't want to burden her, even though she could feel a deep hole opening up under her feet. A hole she expected might have been the same hole that had opened beneath her dad.

Just then, though, her phone began to ring, and she pulled it out of her pocket. It was a video call from Cress.

14

After finishing the hot cup of coffee, Lea went back to her phone and booted it up. She went straight for her camera roll, finding the solitary photo of the lot out back. In the farthest reaches of the phone's weak flash, she could make out the concrete foundation where the street address was crudely spray-painted in orange. The unfinished building was there.

That morning, after hooking Wyvern into his harness, she took him toward Forest and saw, down south, where she'd watched the building eat her neighbour's house, a fire truck. The truck's lights were silently spinning. Some neighbours were on the street, wearing coats over pyjamas, just like her the night before. She directed Wyvern down that way, and as they got close, she saw the firefighters gathered on the lawn in front of a house that had burned nearly to the ground.

"What happened?" Lea asked one of the neighbours standing on the sidewalk, who was deep in the steam of a huge mug of coffee.

"Gas leak, apparently," she said, glancing over at Lea and smiling a little when she noticed Wyvern. "Thank God no one was home."

Lea and Wyvern stood there, in the silent flashing of the fire truck's lights, watching firefighters carry waterlogged belongings from the wreckage of the house. She realized, standing there and looking at all the remaining houses nearby, that the burned house was one she'd always found beautiful, because it had been infested with ivy so thick that the north side of the house was hardly visible. She remembered a satellite dish on the roof wound with vines, indecipherable from the cables that carried whatever signal the dish could grab. She thought, for the first time, that probably the vines of that ivy had ruined their reception, pulling it slowly away from its calibration. Then she remembered watching the dish being plucked off the house like a garnish and dropped into a gaping concrete maw.

At work that day, between the morning hours and afternoon hours of her sophomore studio, Lea took lunch in the cafeteria, sketching the building in her sketchbook while her food got cold. The sketch was crude, scratchy, and frightening. As she put the pen down she looked up to see Harper carrying a tray. Lea smiled at her.

"Can I join you, Professor Jensen?" Harper asked, from behind her mask. Lea was alone at the table, one of the few with only a single person sitting at it.

"Of course, Harper. So long as you call me Lea."

"Roger, roger, Lea," Harper said, saluting and then sitting down at the table a little cattywampus from Lea, then taking off her paper mask. Lea caught herself staring a bit at Harper, who was carefully moving things around on her plate and whose face Lea realized she'd never fully seen before. As Lea caught herself and averted her eyes, Harper looked over at Lea's sketchbook.

"Is that a sketch of your next piece?" Harper asked, angling her fork in her very pale, thin fingers.

"Oh," Lea said, looking down at the sketch. "I suppose it could be. It's just something that I've … that I've been seeing in my dreams."

"'The strangest inspirations come from the most everyday of places,'" Harper said, stabbing at a cherry tomato, which rolled off her plate and onto the floor. Her immaculately painted eyes widened, and her lips pursed, transforming her into a key frame in a cartoon before she began going after another tomato on her plate, more gently this time.

"I said that, didn't I?" Lea asked, suddenly embarrassed at the sound of her own voice.

"Roger, roger."

That afternoon, as Lea helped one of her students make a plan of attack on reworking their midterm project for the end-of-semester show, she thought about the building. The memory made her feel insane, particularly how deeply sensory the experience had been. If it *had* been a dream, which she wanted to believe, it was as lucid and real a dream as she'd ever had.

She remembered the cold, the crunch, the wet air on her skin, the wind—both ambient wind and the disturbed air from the movement of the building's huge arms as it sheared studs from the wall to slurp like pasta.

As she finished up with her student and wandered toward her desk, she suddenly remembered something new: the building finishing its feast, then turning toward her. In the building, where a person's heart would be, she saw a piece of the concrete foundation, with rebar splitting out like arteries. She'd been transfixed by this point in its chest as it began to spark, began to dance with bright light snaking out like lightning, until finally the building took a step toward her, and a spark from its heart reached out to Lea, and everything went white.

Lea had a hand on her desk, propping herself up, while her other hand hovered at the place where she'd been struck. The spot, where belly met breast, was tender, and she excused herself to the bathroom, where she lifted up her shirt, facing the mirror. There was nothing there.

But when she looked down at her body unreflected, she saw a subtle dark lightning-shaped figure blooming from the centre of the point of contact.

15

In the video call, Lea learned that Castro had told Cress about Lea's dad when they'd run into each other at a bar in the Crossroads. Cress said she'd called to say that she was sorry—sorry about Lea's dad, and sorry for how fucked up she'd treated Lea before. Lea didn't really know what to do, what to say. She didn't want to forgive Cress, and so she didn't. But she let Cress keep talking to her anyway. She let Cress keep calling her back.

Whenever they told the story of their relationship, Lea and Cress only ever identified the beginning as the meet-cute in the bar, when they'd played pool together. They didn't talk about how Lea won two of the three games because Cress kept sinking the eight ball out of order, or that Cress became blackout drunk by the last game—something Lea herself did not know until she texted Cress a few days after, wondering if she wanted to hang out again. Depending on the audience, Lea would sometimes talk about how she had incidentally looked up Cress's skirt, and how that had awakened something that had, for a very long time, seemed determined to stay dormant.

They never talked about the breakup, the concealment of Cress's messy divorce, or the way that Lea's trust was reshaped by the caustic animosity she had lived with over the course of that year, whose ghost would occasionally meander into the room. They never talked about Lea's dad dying, or the girls from Connecticut Lea met with on dating apps—it was technically not far away, despite being across the Long Island Sound—who were interested enough to get her hopes up, but not interested enough to let Lea take a ferry to meet them. They didn't talk about how

Lea and Cress started video calling almost every night. How Lea once said she needed to go take a shower, and Cress said, "Well, take me with you," and so Lea propped her phone against a roll of toilet paper so Cress could watch. Or how apparently Cress had a few times secretly masturbated while listening to Lea tell various boring stories about drama among the graduate students. None of that, none of those years that Lea was away for graduate school, ever came up in their story. Instead, they presented to folks an unbroken line.

In the summer of 2018, Lea made a trip back to Kansas City. She stayed with Castro, who had just broken up with their long-time partner. "Fuck 'em," they said, on the drive back from the airport.

Cress and Lea met up, for the first time in more than a year, at a house party in Waldo. Cress gave Lea a long hug, and they chatted for a bit—nervous and awkward without the slight latency they'd grown accustomed to—before splitting off to separate groups. At the end of the night, Lea drove a very intoxicated Castro home, and Castro kept asking her, as they nodded off and on, if she was going to go see Cress after she dropped them off. Lea said no, of course not. Instead, she spent the next few hours silently gagging as she rubbed Castro's heaving back in the bathroom.

They didn't end up having sex again until Christmas, when Lea came back into town to spend the holidays with Castro and their family. She and Cress met up at the same bar where they'd originally met, since Cress lived nearby, and got fairly drunk, then wandered to Cress's apartment—both underdressed and holding hands in the shivering dark. A few hours later, sobered, Lea walked back to the car and drove back to Castro's.

Even so, they didn't call what they were doing dating. Lea went back to school and kept talking to girls on apps, some of whom finally decided to meet up with her in person. She felt as if fucking Cress over that break had somehow freed her. She casually dated a few women, but none of them could match the inexplicable hold that Cress had on her. They still talked most nights, shared stories of their various dates, talked about potential visits that mostly didn't happen. But some of them did.

The summer before her last year, Lea got a two-week residency in the Flint Hills of Kansas, where she worked on a new sculpture called *The Condemnation of Adam*. The organization who hosted the residency helped coordinate space and resources at a shop in Matfield Green that had the welders and acetylene torches she needed to fabricate her sculpture—a hand, in as Michelangelo-esque a rendering as she could accomplish with bent metal, pointing a jagged, furious finger at the sky, as if condemning the heavens for man's creation. At the end of the residency, the sculpture was still somewhat crude but finished enough, and they installed it on the top of a hill that overlooked a public art path in Matfield Green. Cress drove up at the end of the residency, at Lea's invitation, and stood nearby and watched as she pounded the metal stake into the few feet of soil that topped the limestone hill. Lea did her best to hold in the waves of grief—its shame, its guilt—that followed the sound of her hammer on the stake. Eventually, she connected the stake to the sculpture, and the shop owner lifted the huge hand up with the prongs of the tractor they'd hauled it there with and placed it atop the stake. Lea wiped away the few tears that slipped past her defences as if they were beads of sweat.

Her MFA thesis show involved various sculptures similar to *The Condemnation of Adam*, which either cursed the heavens for human suffering or begged the sky for mercy. The answer to both condemnation and mercy was always the same: bolts of energy a billion joules strong, and temperatures several times hotter than the surface of the sun. In her presentation of the thesis paper that accompanied her final portfolio, which she gave over Zoom in April of 2020, Lea said that the uniformity of the response to her work was what interested her most about it. That no matter what she made, her pieces seemed to be treated indiscriminately by the lightning as interchangeable conduits for their massive charges to pass through. As a way to neutralize discord between the heavens and the earth. That no matter what, the heavens—or nature itself, as Lea began to frame it—spoke *something* through her art. She said, in her closing remarks, "Perhaps there is nuance in these replies, in the strikes on my work, but from my perspective, they all look the same. But perhaps it is simply a failure on our part to be able to understand the nuances in nature's speech."

After she picked up her diploma that summer, Lea moved from Port Jefferson into Cress's little apartment. Lea had been offered some adjunct work by her former mentor at the art institute, now that she had her MFA. She'd planned to crash with Castro while she looked for a place, but Castro, having met a man from Los Angeles at a fashion show and moved there to be with him a few weeks before Lea came back to the city—pandemic be damned—was no longer an option. Lea never planned to *stay* with Cress when she moved back to the city, but given the fact that they were going to create a pandemic bubble together anyway, she did.

And so their story climbed onto the rails that they would later pretend it had always been on.

But neither Lea nor Cress realized that their circling back to one another—talking, then visiting, then fucking, then moving in together—had all started with Cress asking Lea for forgiveness, which Lea never gave. Cress never asked for it again, and Lea never thought to offer it. Instead, the ask existed somewhere between them, a Schrödinger's forgiveness that, unobserved, was simultaneously given and not. A difference in charge, singing in the foundations of them.

16

When Lea got home after finding the little lightning figure on her chest, she found Cress sitting at the dining room table, her witch's box open. She was opening various vials, checking the contents, making inventory of what she needed replaced. After glancing up at Lea, who was standing next to the table, watching her, Cress reached into the box and pulled out a thin, curvy, bleached bone—a baculum, a raccoon's penis bone—and winked at her.

Not getting a laugh, Cress asked, "How was work?"

"It was okay," Lea said, taking a step closer and placing her lips on the crown of Cress's head. "Did you have any clients today?"

"Yeah, one," Cress said, lifting out the little cauldron of chicken bones and placing it next to the box, beside her mortar and pestle. "But he cancelled, so I've been doing some fall inventory, as I want to make sure I'm set for Halloween. It's been a quiet fall so far, but I'm a little low on black salt."

"Can you look at something for me?" Lea asked, and by the time Cress turned her head, Lea's shirt was hiked up just below her tiny, braless breasts. Cress leaned away in the chair, staring, a finger on her bright, pursed lips. After a few moments, she leaned forward as if to take a closer look before kissing Lea in the spot where the figure spidered out, wrapping her hands around Lea's body, and slowly nudging the shirt higher with her nose as she kissed her way to Lea's left nipple.

After Lea finally slid down the far end of her orgasm, the first they'd shared together in nearly two months, Cress slid up next to her, pressing her body against Lea's in the cool air of the bedroom. In the living room, Wyvern's toy squawked, begging for its life from between his merciless terrier jaws. As Lea's heart rate normalized, she sat up a little and looked down at the dark figure on her chest. She pointed at it.

"So you don't see anything here?" Lea asked Cress, who sat up a little as well, actually inspecting the spot this time.

"You were serious about that?" Cress asked, sitting up fully, her cold-ringed nipples blaring as she leaned in to take an actual look. "I thought you were just making a move. But I don't see anything. Does it hurt?"

"No," Lea said, wanting to try and open the space between them, to be vulnerable about the things that had been manifesting to her—but she found those words immovable. "It just feels funny, I guess."

That week, Lea began assessing how she could approach making her sketch of the building into an actual sculpture. She made lists of things she'd need—rebar, concrete, timber—and began trying to think of ways she could make manifest that arcing in its chest, which she'd began to think of as the somewhat-rare lightning phenomenon known as St. Elmo's fire.

On Halloween, Lea and Cress and Wyvern all went over to a friend's house in Old Hyde Park, a few blocks from Janssen Place, and hung out next to a firepit as their friends handed out candy to heavily layered trick-or-treaters. It was the coldest Halloween on record for Kansas City, and the cold—alongside the general sense of the world crumbling, particularly regarding the ongoing genocide in Palestine—meant that neither Lea nor Cress had mustered the energy to come up with costumes to wear. Wyvern was the only one of the three who wore a costume, his perennial skeleton onesie.

That night, Lea, for the first time in a long time, excused herself from conversations again and again to pull out her pocket notebook from her parka and make indecipherable scribbles inside. As she stood there—Wyvern sitting on her foot so as to avoid having to sit on the freezing blacktop driveway—thinking of the unfinished building stalking the streets, she was happy to be away from it. She was happy to be in a completely different neighbourhood, which was far too fancy to allow those trashy new-build houses to sprout, and really only meant that the neighbourhood had long since established itself as an impenetrable white space.

As she thought of her own little neighbourhood, just east of Troost Avenue, Lea quickly pulled out the notebook one last time to scrawl the title that would finally set her decision to make the sculpture into motion: *St. (J.C.) Nichols's fire?*

17

Early in the fall of 2020, as Lea's first semester teaching at the art institute began—on hard mode, as she would be teaching sculpture virtually—she actively looked at apartments. Just as she was trying to decide between two different places, both a little beyond her budget, Cress told Lea that she wanted to get a dog.

Cress's work in touch therapy was severely impacted by the ongoing pandemic, and she was getting a little stir crazy. Though she collected unemployment, she spent most of her time on Zoom, doing tarot readings and various other rituals virtually. While Cress gave insights into the future of mostly bored white women in her little sunroom office space, Lea sat at the kitchen table, trying to discuss the importance of considering the unique material physics of the mediums of sculpture, staring at a zoning grid of anywhere from six to eight tired pixelated faces.

One Saturday, over coffee, Cress told Lea that she had an appointment at a shelter in Grandview to look at dogs.

"I just can't live here alone," she said. "If I let myself do that, I'll fall right off the face of the earth."

On the drive to Grandview, Lea scrolled through photos of the two apartments on her phone. One was a few blocks from work, which worried her because she might end up living far too close to some of her students, and the other was maybe a mile from where Cress lived, cost hundreds more than her half of the rent with Cress, and would involve two other roommates. But something inside her told her that she needed the space, that it was too soon, too much to live with Cress. That there was still healing they needed to do, and being on top of one another would not allow that to happen. That being together would force their individual wounds to scab over into one scar, shackling two hurting bodies into one.

But by the end of that day, she decided to stay with Cress. When they got to the shelter, after donning their cotton masks, they were guided into a room that held rows and rows of dogs. Something had happened before they arrived, and when they walked in it seemed like every single dog in the room—if not the planet—was barking at once. They walked past howling pit bulls, loud labs, and yappy chihuahuas until they finally walked past a small twenty-pound, five-year-old black terrier mix named Collin, who was sitting in his cage, panting and unbothered.

In the quieter little chain-linked yard connected to the complex, Lea and Cress met Collin. Cress talked to the employee, asking about his history and the adoption costs, but Lea didn't bother to listen to any of that. Instead, she walked Collin around, tossed some tennis balls for him, and fell into an unfathomable love with the creature.

They didn't take Collin home, but they did put a hold on him. On the drive home, they talked about it. Cress wasn't quite as sure, thinking perhaps they should keep looking, but Lea said, "I want him."

"*You* want him?" Cress asked, glancing over at Lea and smiling. "I thought I was the one getting a dog!"

"Well then, I want *you* to get him, but I want to live with him."

Two hours later, Cress called the shelter and told them they wanted Collin. On the drive back to Grandview, they tried to think of new names for the dog. After a few minutes of back and forth, Lea asked, "Why not something a little bit monstrous?"

As they pulled up and got out of Cress's car, masking up, they had found a name: Wyvern, the name of a class of mythical two-legged dragonlike creatures. They finished the paperwork, paid, and drove Wyvern home, their wounds continuing to weave their fibrous tissues together, binding them into their own two-legged creature.

18

After Halloween, Lea found herself slipping into the usual slump with her students—frustrated by their fall-off in energy, annoyed that she'd ever believed adjunct teaching was a sustainable practice. Every semester, around the same two-thirds point, Lea felt that she was not so much a teacher anymore, but rather some kind of prison guard. Every reading or assignment she gave to her students was met with a wall of silent exhaustion. It felt, somehow, violent to ask anything of them, just as it felt violent whenever things began to be asked of her. This point of the semester always made clear how little support she had, how thin the ties she had with the rest of the institution. It always became most clear to her that she was replaceable, that there was no true permanence to her role—aside from the care of her department head—and that there was no foundation upon which she could build her presence in the institution into something more impactful to her students and herself. She just taught her sophomores, then inherited new ones, never building relationships that spanned much longer than a year.

She floated alongside the institution, a dissonant charge building inside her, rather than being a healthy part of its circuit.

But this semester, at least, she had a project that was forming inside of her and which was finally starting to manifest in the real world as well. While she gave grace to old deadlines and reiterated the firmness of the deadline for their final project, which would be exhibited at the end-of-semester show, Lea took trips to Home Depot and scrounged Facebook Marketplace for scrap rebar, two-by-fours, and other building materials. Over her lunch breaks, she spent time in the general shop on campus, fabricating moulds for the concrete of the mouth and the limbs of the building, which she planned to build at a 1:3 scale, such that it would stand at about nine feet tall. For those around Lea's height—five foot six—this would place the eventually sparking heart at eye level.

The nights that followed the ivy-riddled house on Forest burning down, the first few nights of November, were quiet, and the days were filled with crews dismantling the ruined structure and others stapling flyers to light posts asking for donations to support the homeowners in replacing their belongings. Behind Lea's house, the unfinished building seemed to stay put, and work continued as if she hadn't seen, less than a week before, the building cat the allegedly burned house to the ground.

Lea bundled up on the cold mornings before work and started walking Wyvern past the site again, trying her best to take notes on how it was progressing and what she needed to add to make her sculpture more believable. Some mornings, walking past the site—when the little Kubota loader was moving rock around the back of the site, or the workers were inside the building and preparing for the second-floor walls to be put in before the roof frames could be lowered atop—Lea would let Wyvern pee on the porta-potty out front. Once, she gave a peace sign to the newly replaced security camera stuck to the tree as he did so.

The hardest thing about the sculpture, aside from trying to figure out how to combine wood and rebar, or even which electronics she would use to try to set up the sparking heart, was the cost of the materials. Being only an adjunct at the institute alienated her from much of the funding her colleagues had access to, which meant that she relied on selling work, or outside grants, or—her least favourite—asking Cress to absorb more of the household costs than she already was. Cress was very supportive of Lea's work and had never said no to such a request, but this wasn't the comfort to Lea that it should have been. It made her feel frivolous.

On the Saturday after Halloween, November 4, Lea drove her little hatchback around the city, hitting up various folks who were selling miscellaneous scraps of building materials—particularly lumber, concrete mix, and plywood. The first she visited was the rarest find: someone selling a box of scrap rebar. The pieces were about a foot at the longest, but Lea planned to use them as accents, having already decided to buy some full-length rods of rebar to build out the skeleton of the sculpture. In particular, she thought these pieces could be perfect for the arteries of the sparking concrete heart.

When she got to the modest ranch-style house of the man in Independence selling the rebar, she walked up past a work truck to ring the doorbell. It was a video doorbell, and after a few seconds, a voice cracked out, "I'm ... the garage," which was followed by the garage door opening. When Lea turned toward the garage, she noticed from this new angle that the logo on the side of the truck was very familiar. At that moment, a large man ducked his way out from under the rising garage door. He was tall, bearded, and broad in his thick Carhartt jacket, blowing a big cloud from a combination of the chilly morning and the vape in his big fist.

"Morning," he said, walking over to his truck. "You're after the bar, yeah?"

Lea took a few steps before her mouth began to work, as though she were one of those old toys that gesticulated only when the wheels were pushed along the floor: "Yeah, that's me," she said, recognizing him, by the way he chewed his lip as he let down the tailgate, as well as by the white hard hat that was lying in the truck's bed, as the boss from the building's site.

"Usually we just scrap this, but the amount we got from this site made me think to post it, because who knows? Could maybe buy me a much-needed steak dinner," he said, dragging a soaked cardboard box to the edge of the bed. "It's a little rusty," he added, drawing from the vape and releasing another long, billowing cloud as far from Lea as he could. Lea's heart pounded at the warmth of this gesture. "That okay?"

"Yeah," Lea said, as she picked up a few of the bars with her leather work gloves. Knowing that the rebar might be from the same building that she was trying to portray excited her. Made the steel feel alive. "This is perfect," she added, not looking up at the boss, thrilled but terrified at what phantoms she might see in him.

19

Lea picked up a few more materials from some folks before meeting Cress for brunch at Succotash. That night, she had trouble sleeping again. She'd been feeling increasingly agitated all day, almost getting into a fight with Cress at brunch over what to do over the Thanksgiving break and growing easily annoyed by Wyvern's persistent sniffing on his afternoon walk. She hadn't quite placed the origin of the agitation, but she'd also stopped looking as soon as she sensed that she was approaching the obvious heat—the boss's resemblance to her dad.

As she lay on the far edge of the queen-size bed—Cress lying one Wyvern-ball away from her—a tone began to drain into her head. She hadn't realized how long it had been since hearing it last. She turned toward the ever-blinded window that looked out on the backyard, and against the screen of the venetian slats, she saw shadows begin to dance, and heard a rustling and creaking. By the time she leaned over from the bed to peer through the blinds, the unfinished building was disappearing north down Forest. As she watched, she felt the figure on her chest rustle too and heard the tone grow quieter.

She got up and closed the bedroom door after her. In her little office, she found the pair of jeans she always kept for when she might decide to head to campus at an ungodly hour. She put those jeans on, as well as her parka, turned off the security system, and went out to her car.

Forest was a one-way, but despite that the building was already hulking against the flow of traffic, Lea went one avenue east to Tracy and headed north on that. No street in her neighbourhood had been so ravaged by the awful, expensive new-build houses quite like Tracy, and Lea drove past several of these new houses—cars out front, security lights blaring, Halloween decorations usurped by turkey lawn signs, and the occasional pride flag hanging from a porch. Even in the dark, these buildings clashed with every beautiful old house that still existed on their blocks.

At first, she wasn't quite sure how she might find the building, but as she drove, the tone grew louder and louder, as if she had a compass inside her skull.

The house hadn't gone far. As Lea followed Tracy, the cacophony of the humming escalated, and by the time she slowed down to a crawl—a few houses down from where the building was inspecting an old two-storey house just at the corner, where Tracy's continuity broke, at 39th Street—she noticed that the sound wasn't only coming from the building outside but was resonating from inside her own car as well. The rebar in the box was singing along to the building, whose body was fuller as it began to pummel the two-storey house as though it were a massive hard-boiled egg and the building itself manically hungry. It hit low, and once it had broken its way through, it began rifling around inside, pulling out internal walls and cramming the wood and drywall and wiring into its huge concrete mouth. Once it had broken a huge hole in the first floor, it stuck its whole head into the house in the same way that Wyvern did when he flattened himself to try and grab a rubber squeaky ball that had slipped under the TV stand.

The building feasted voraciously. Horrified, Lea glanced at 39th Street, at her rear-view windows, everywhere, but there were no people, no cars, nothing, it seemed, in the world but her and the house and the blaring song of the rebar. As she slowly pulled

closer, barely realizing she was still moving, the unfinished building paused its chomping inside the house, then pulled its head free
and stood tall. As it turned around, the tone of the rebar was so
loud that Lea almost passed out, and she realized that the building
heard it, too.

She floored the gas pedal just as she saw the building's heart
sparking with the St. Elmo's fire again. The building lunged onto
Tracy, just missing her as she sped through the stop sign onto 39th,
which thankfully was eerily empty. She glanced back to see the
building step onto 39th. In the rear-view mirror she saw it scream
into the sky, the fire in its chest arcing to the rebar all along its
body. But as she swerved onto Troost Avenue and headed back
toward home, she didn't see it follow. The tone quieted. The rebar
in the back seat finally went silent.

When she got back, she parked her car near the end of the
street—near Troost—and left the box of rebar in the back but took
out anything else that seemed important. She felt a dark paranoia
weaving across her chest and up her neck, though once she made
it into the house—setting the security system again—and went to
the bathroom to splash some water on her face, she found that
what she'd felt was actually the dark figure weaving across her
body. She took off her shirt and saw that the figure had spread,
looking like a combination of lightning paused in the sky and the
branching fingers of a fungus.

She didn't go back to bed. Instead, she returned to the attic and
moved her chair back to the window. She looked out there all night
long, and woke up to Cress shaking her shoulder and Wyvern tilting his head up at her.

"What are you doing?" Cress asked, brow furrowed. Lea's neck was a single knot. "Why are you up here?"

Lea didn't answer right away. She stiffly turned her head to the window, where the unfinished building had returned.

"I don't know," she said, which felt like the most honest sentence she'd placed between them in a very long time. "I don't know."

20

The morning following the chase, Lea stood in the kitchen massaging the crick in her neck as Cress finished grinding the coffee beans, added them to the steel French press, and poured the hot water in. After setting a timer on the microwave, she turned around.

"So, it's just that you've been seeing this scary house in your dreams, right?" Cress asked, leaning against the counter. Wyvern was crunching his breakfast near the back door.

"I guess," Lea said, looking down at her left hand, where the dark lines of the figure had snaked all the way down to her wrist. "Sort of. They don't feel like dreams, and the first time, something bad happened to the house that it ate."

"Okay," Cress said, her voice thinning out in its confidence. "Maybe they're, like, visions. Like, you feel ... you're maybe being activated as a sort of conduit for some dark energy?"

Lea was quiet, staring down at her hand, tilting her neck back and forth to try and free it from the ache. She realized in that moment that the building's animation had changed her perspective on Cress's beliefs about energies, and she wondered—and hoped—that perhaps Cress was right. But her silence in response did not, to Cress, endorse the idea.

"I know, I know," Cress said, turning around to the French press, minutes still remaining until it was time to plunge. "But I do think there are certain places, certain nodes, where dark energy spills out into our world. Maybe all the negativity behind this building being built allowed that to break through. And it found you somehow receptive to its signal and is trying to use you to warn people that something bad is going to happen to those houses."

"Well," Lea said, "I'm not sure anything has happened to that last house."

After the timer went off and the coffee was plunged and divided into two travel mugs, they buckled Wyvern into his harness and went out to Lea's car. The car wasn't parked where she'd left it the night before, nearer to Troost, but when she went around to the driver's side as Cress opened the back door to Wyvern, who leapt in excitedly, Lea saw deep scratches on the paint below the rear window of the hatchback. She put her fingers on the scratches and looked into the back window, at the cardboard box full of the rusting pieces of rebar. She didn't say anything to Cress. She felt the branching figure move restlessly against her body for a moment before growing still. Reminding her.

Lea followed the same path she'd taken the night before, only this time she had to stop for pedestrians, squirrels, and cars passing on crossroads. There was life again. As they got to the last block of Tracy, they saw that the rest of the street was blocked off to through traffic. They pulled over, got Wyvern from the car, and walked with their coffees toward 39th Street.

At the end of the block they found neighbours circling the lot, and as they got closer they saw that someone in a big green pickup truck had careened off of 39th directly into the ground floor of the house.

On the drive back to their place, they didn't say much of anything, their minds boarding separate trains of thought, Lea's being that it was only a matter of time until the building came after her. That somehow, all the instability throughout her life—work, love, family—had led to this moment, when one bad house with one bad foundation would finally finish her off.

Lea did not imagine what Cress was thinking. Cress did not share; Lea did not ask.

Later that day, just before dinner, Cress had to leave for a dinner party followed by a ceremony she would be doing with a polycule of her friends in Waldo, some of whom were the friends who'd hosted the party where Lea and Cress met again after they'd originally broken up. Lea helped carry Cress's wooden witch's box to her little Honda, while Cress carried her straw broom along-side a small broom and dustpan, which she used to try and save as much of the old dirt she liked to use for drawing pentagrams or circles.

"Everything is gonna be all right," Cress said, hugging Lea. "I'll be back late, or I may have to stay the night, okay?" Cress squeezed a little harder. "You know how these gays guzzle."

"I know," Lea said.

After Cress had driven off, Lea went over to her car and fin-gered the gouges on the hatchback again. She imagined a massive concrete face nuzzling the door, like the T. Rex from *Jurassic Park*. Somehow, it felt as if the building knew where she was. That it would be coming back for her.

Before it got too late, Lea went to the basement, to the long box she had always avoided opening, because what it held had too much power: the rusty old lightning rod she and her father had made, which she had uninstalled from the edge of the potato field and put into a storage unit Lars had rented in Roseau before leaving for New York. Beside the stake was also her dad's mini sledgehammer, which he'd used to install it.

Lea felt the dark figure stretching and coiling along her body as she carried the main rod, the grounding rod, and the mini sledge out into the yard. The earth was cold, but thankfully temperatures were rarely freezing during the night, so she was optimistic she would be able to get the stake into the earth. Her phone went off in her pocket—photos of the spread at Cress's ceremony—as she knelt on the damp front yard, hammering the stake into the ground. Wyvern watched from the other side of the mesh security door.

Afterward, she put a frozen Costco pizza in the oven, then went to her office and grabbed a ballpoint pen. She set her phone up in the kitchen, the front-facing camera facing her, then took off her shirt and hit Record.

"This is what I see," Lea said, and the video showed a topless Lea standing against the counter covered in dirty dishes, looking down at her chest and drawing lines out from the middle of her chest with the blue ballpoint pen. They stretched from her belly to the tips of her fingers. They branched off from one another like blood vessels, like rivers, like lightning desperate to find its ground. The video was fourteen minutes long, and Lea cut herself off only because the timer for the pizza went off.

After she ate two-thirds of the pizza and sat down on the couch with Wyvern, her heart pounding, she uploaded the video to the cloud and put a link to it in an email, which she scheduled to deliver the next day. She didn't want to scare Cress—or she didn't want her to come back. She wept, sitting there, thinking about all the distance and discord between her and so many elements of her world, about the discord in every piece of the world she lived in, about the pain and violence in the foundations of it all. Even Wyvern, a rescue and probably the purest thing she had in her life, had things in his own raising that had permanently destroyed his ability to be a functional creature in the world.

Just before midnight, Lea got dressed in her parka, went to her car and pulled out the box of rebar, and set it on the lawn beside the lightning rod. She didn't set the rod upright but let it lie on its side on the lawn, tethered to the grounding rod by three feet of wire. She sat on the lawn beside it.

Eventually, the night went quiet, and behind her—behind her own house—she heard the tone rising, followed by the tone of the trimmed rebar in the box rising into harmony with it. She breathed in and out and watched as the unfinished building came around from Forest, walking up to the gap where Cress's car would normally be. It was so tall, and so much more full, now that it was nearing completion—perhaps only days away from having its roof attached, Lea had estimated the last time she looked at the site. The tone grew loud, shaking Lea's skull as she stood up on the lawn, taking up space between the house and the box of rebar and the animated building.

As complete as it was, there was still a huge gap in its chest where the big concrete heart was set. She could see, as it took a step closer to her, that the concrete heart was beating, and then the St. Elmo's fire began to rage in its chest again.

As its huge lumber hands opened wide and it lunged toward her, Lea braced herself and lifted the lightning rod, feeling the figure on her body explode into warmth as the rod made contact with the heart, and the white fire bathed every inch of Lea's world.

Acknowledgments

I would like to offer thanks to some folks:

To the team over at Arsenal Pulp, for continuing to find room for me in one of the best publishing houses in the business, and for helping to make this book its best self, and for getting it into your hands.

To all the editors who previously published earlier versions of these stories.

To the writers and artists who offered their endorsements for this book. It's a gift to be able to put the names of people I admire on my book.

To my little Kansas City writing group, for their careful eyes over the years. Some of these stories may never have made the cut without your encouragement.

To Brian Suarez, for your generous and helpful early read of "Blueness."

To Dominik Parisien, for the feedback that helped give a final shape to "Moving Parts," and for later giving it a home in *Plenitude*.

To Axel B. Kolcow, champion of my short fiction, for reading so many of these stories before anyone else. Nobody wanted this book to exist as much as you.

To Melanie Pierce, for all your love and support over these (many!) weird years. Through the forward dark.

To Grendel, for being an inspiration, and for being the best little friend a girl could have.

To my parents, for working so hard to make an impossible life like mine possible. I would never have been able to dream my dreams without you. To my brothers, for helping me fall in love with telling stories in that damp, dark crawl space. I would be nothing without those decades of practice.

And finally, thank you to all the folks who have spent time with my work over the last decade, and to any of you for whom *Bad Houses* is your introduction. My words have personal lives because of you, and that's all I could ever ask for. May we all build a better house together.

JOHN ELIZABETH STINTZI (they/she) is a writer, cartoonist, photographer, and editor who grew up on a cattle farm in northwestern Ontario. Their work has been awarded the 2019 RBC Bronwen Wallace Award for Emerging Writers, *The Malahat Review*'s 2019 Long Poem Prize, and the 2020 Sator New Works Award. JES is the author of the novels *My Volcano* (longlisted for the Brooklyn Public Library Book Prize for fiction and named a book of the year by *Kirkus Reviews* and the New York Public Library) and *Vanishing Monuments* (shortlisted for the Amazon Canada First Novel Award), as well as the poetry collection *Junebat*.

johnelizabethstintzi.com